"Eva, I'm going to do everything in my power to find Brady," Austin said.

He held her gaze. "I promise you that. I know your son was in these woods. I know exactly where Justice lost the scent trail, and I feel confident that he can find it again, but not if we don't go look for it."

"Okay," Eva said. He was right. Talking only wasted energy that could be spent finding Brady.

"Great. You can wait in your car or go back to your place. As soon as we have new information—"

"No."

"What?" He stopped short, his eyes flashing with irritation, Justice tugging hard on the lead.

"I'm coming with you, Detective."

TEXAS K-9 UNIT:

These lawmen solve the toughest cases with the help of their brave canine partners

Books by Shirlee McCoy

Love Inspired Suspense

Die Before Nightfall
Even in the Darkness
When Silence Falls
Little Girl Lost
Valley of Shadows
Stranger in the Shadows
Missing Persons
Lakeview Protector
*The Guardian's Mission
*The Protector's Promise
Cold Case Murder
*The Defender's Duty
†Running for Cover
Deadly Vows
†Running Scared

†Running Blind
Out of Time
†Lone Defender
†Private Eye Protector
The Lawman's Legacy
†Undercover Bodyguard
†Navy SEAL Rescuer
Tracking Justice

Love Inspired Single Title

Still Waters

*The Sinclair Brothers
†Heroes for Hire

SHIRLEE McCOY

has always loved making up stories. As a child, she day-dreamed elaborate tales in which she was the heroine—gutsy, strong and invincible. Though she soon grew out of her superhero fantasies, her love for storytelling never diminished. She knew early that she wanted to write inspirational fiction, and she began writing her first novel when she was a teenager. Still, it wasn't until her third son was born that she truly began pursuing her dream of being published. Three years later, she sold her first book. Now a busy mother of five, Shirlee is a homeschool mom by day and an inspirational author by night. She and her husband and children live in the Pacific Northwest and share their house with a dog, two cats and a bird. You can visit her website, www.shirleemccoy.com, or email her at shirlee@shirleemccoy.com.

SHIRLEE McCOY

TRACKING JUSTICE

Love Inspired

Special thanks and acknowledgment to Shirlee McCoy for her contribution to the Texas K-9 Unit miniseries.

Recycling programs for this product may not exist in your area.

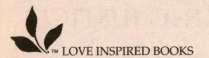

™ LOVE INSPIRED BOOKS

ISBN-13: 978-0-373-67541-8

TRACKING JUSTICE

Restore to me the joy of your salvation
and grant me a willing spirit, to sustain me.
—*Psalm* 51:12

Much thanks to extraordinary editor,
Emily Rodmell. Without your guidance and expertise
(and patience), this book would not be what it is.

And to the K-9 Justice continuity authors—
Sharon Dunn, Lenora Worth, Terri Reed,
Valerie Hansen and Margaret Daley—
I loved working with every one of you!
Thank you for your kindness and encouragement
after my accident. It meant the world to me.

ONE

Police detective Austin Black glanced at the illuminated numbers on the dashboard clock as he raced up Oak Drive. Two in the morning. Not a good time to get a call about a missing child.

Then again, there was never a good time for that; never a good time to look in the eyes of a mother or father and see terror and worry or to follow a scent trail and know that it might lead to a joyful reunion or a sorrowful goodbye.

If it led anywhere.

Sometimes trails went cold, scents were lost and the missing were never found.

Knowing that didn't make it any easier to accept.

Austin wanted to find them all. Bring them all home safe.

Hopefully, this time, he would.

He pulled into the driveway of a small, bungalow-style house, its white porch gleaming in exterior lights that glowed on either side of the door.

Just four houses down from the scene of a violent crime and the theft of a trained police dog the previous afternoon. An odd coincidence.

Or maybe not.

Two calls to the same street within nine hours? Not something that happened often in a place like Sagebrush, Texas.

Justice whined, his dark nose pressed against the grate that separated him from the SUV's backseat. A three-year-old bloodhound, he was trained in search and rescue and knew when it was time to work. Knew and was ready, even after the eight-hour search they'd been on earlier.

Austin jumped out of the vehicle and started up the driveway, filing away information as he went. Lights on in the front of the house. An old station wagon parked on the curb. Windows closed. Locked?

A woman darted out the front door, pale hair flowing behind her, a loose robe flapping in the cold night air as she ran toward him. "Thank God you got here so quickly. I don't know where he could have gone."

"You called about a missing child?"

"Yes. My son."

"The dispatcher said that you don't know how long he's been gone?" Austin had heard the call go out shortly after he'd left his captain's place. Hours of searching for Slade's stolen police dog,

Rio, had turned up nothing but a dead-end scent trail and mounting frustration. Austin had been exhausted and ready to go home. Now he felt wired and ready to hit the trail again.

"I thought that I heard Brady call for me, and when I walked into his room, he was gone. That was about ten minutes ago."

"Has he ever run away?"

"No."

"Ever talked about it?"

"No! Now, please, can you help me find him?" She ran back up the porch stairs, her bare feet padding on the whitewashed wood.

Austin jogged after her, stepping into a small living room. Neat as a pin except for a small pile of Legos on a light oak coffee table and a college textbook abandoned on a threadbare sofa. No sign of the woman.

"Ma'am?" he called, moving toward a narrow hallway that led toward the back of the house.

"Here." She waved from a doorway at the end of the hall. "This is my son's room."

Austin followed her into the tiny room. Blue walls. Blue bedding tangled and dripping over the side of the twin mattress. Crisp white curtains. A blanket lay on the floor near the open window, the frayed edges ruffled by the wind.

"How old is your son, Ms…?"

"Billows. Eva. He's seven."

Billows?

The name sparked a memory, but Austin couldn't quite grab hold of it. "Did you and your son have an argument about something? Maybe a missed curfew or—"

"He's *seven*. He's not even allowed to be outside by himself." Her voice broke, but her eyes were dry, her face pale and pinched with worry. A pretty face. A young one, too. Maybe twenty-three or four. Too young, it seemed, to have a seven-year-old.

"Did you argue about homework? Grades?"

"We didn't argue about anything, Officer—?"

"Detective Austin Black. I'm with Sagebrush Police Department's Special Operations K-9 Unit."

"You have a search-and-rescue dog with you?" Her face brightened, hope gleaming in her emerald eyes. "I can give you something of his. A shirt or—"

"Hold on." He grabbed her arm as she tried to move past. "I need to get a little more information first."

"Find my son. *Then* I'll give you whatever information you want."

"Unfortunately, without the information, I won't know where to begin searching for your son."

"How about you start out there?" She gestured out the window.

"Was it open when you came in the room?"

"Yes. And the curtains were just like that. One hanging outside. Like, maybe…" She pressed her lips together.

"What?"

"It looks like someone carried Brady out the window, and Brady grabbed the curtain to try to keep from being taken. But I don't know how anyone could have gotten into his room. The window was locked. *All* the doors and windows were locked."

He nodded. He could see the scenario she'd outlined playing out. The little boy woken from a sound sleep, dragged from his bed and out the window, grabbing on to whatever he could to keep from being kidnapped.

He could see it, but that didn't mean it had happened that way. Most children were abducted by family or friends, and most didn't even know they were being abducted when it happened.

"You're sure everything was locked?"

"Of course." She frowned. "I always double-check. I have ever since…"

"What?"

"Nothing that matters. I just need to find my son."

Hiding something?

Maybe. She seemed more terrified than nervous, but that didn't mean she didn't know something about what had happened to her son.

"Everything matters when a child is missing, Eva."

Missing.

Gone.

Disappeared.

The words just kept coming. Kept filling Eva's head and her heart and her lungs until she wasn't sure she could breathe.

"Do you need to sit down?" Detective Black touched her elbow, his dark blue eyes staring straight into hers.

"I need to find my son." The words stuck in her throat, caught on the roof of her mouth, and she didn't know if they even made a sound when they escaped through her lips.

"I'm going to help you do that. I promise. But I need to know if there's some reason why you were careful to keep your doors and windows locked. Someone you were afraid of." His voice was warm and smooth as honey straight from the hive, and Eva might actually believe every word he was saying if she weren't so terrified.

"My parents were killed two years ago, but it had nothing to do with me or my son."

"The killer was caught?"

"No."

"Is it possible—"

"It's not possible!" She nearly shouted, and Detective Black frowned. "I was estranged from my father when the murders occurred. There's no connection between my life now and what happened to my parents." She tried again. Tried to sound reasonable and responsible because she was afraid if she didn't, the detective would linger in Brady's room for hours instead of going to look for him.

"Is Brady's father around?" He leaned out the window without touching it, eyeing the packed earth beneath.

Did he see anything there?

She wanted to ask, wanted to beg him to get his dog and go after her son, wanted to go after Brady herself, run into the darkness and scream his name over and over again until she found him.

"No," she answered a little too sharply, and Detective Black raised a raven-black eyebrow.

"You're not on good terms?"

"We're not on any terms."

"When was the last time you and Brady saw him?"

"Brady has never seen him," she retorted. "The last time I saw Rick was six months before my son was born."

"Have you spoken to him on th—"

"I haven't had any contact with him since the day I told him I was pregnant. He's not in my life.

He's not in Brady's life. He didn't want to be. He was married, okay? He and his wife moved to Las Vegas two months before Brady's birth. That's it. The whole story." She'd been nineteen and foolish enough to believe every lie Rick had told. It didn't hurt like it used to, but admitting it to the detective still made her blush.

"Is there anyone else? A boyfriend? Fiancé?"

"No. Just me and Brady. That's all there's ever been." She swallowed hard and turned away. Holding back tears because crying wouldn't solve her problems. Wouldn't help her son.

"When did you last see Brady?"

"I checked on him at midnight. Right before I went to bed. He was sleeping."

"You went to bed after that?"

"Yes! I went to bed. I fell asleep. I thought I heard Brady call for me, and I went to his room. He was gone. Now, will you please go find him?"

"I will. A soon as—"

The doorbell rang and Eva jumped, her heart soaring with wild hope.

Brady.

Please, God, let it be him.

She shoved past Detective Black, not caring about niceties. Not caring about anything but getting to the door, opening it, seeing Brady's face.

Only it wasn't him.

Her heart sank as she looked into the eyes of a uniformed officer.

"Ms. Billows? I'm Officer Desmond Cunningham. We have a report of a missing child?"

"My son. There's already a detective here."

"He's with our K-9 Unit. He'll start searching for your son while I interview you."

Thank You, God. Thank You, thank You, thank You.

She stepped back so he could enter the house, wishing she'd had time to straighten up the living room, put the sofa cover over her threadbare couch. A twenty-dollar Goodwill find that worked fine for her and Brady but wasn't great for company.

Such a silly thing to think about.

Such a stupid thing when her son was missing.

She pressed a hand to her stomach, sick with dread and fear.

"He's been gone for twenty minutes already," she said, the horror of the words filling her mouth with the coppery taste of blood.

"It takes a little time to get a search team mobilized, ma'am, but we'll have plenty of people out here before you know it." Officer Cunningham offered a reassuring smile, his dark eyes filled with sympathy.

Seeing it there in the depth of his gaze was too difficult, made the tears she'd been holding back too tempting. She turned away, met Detective Black's steady gaze.

Deep blue. Bottomless. Unreadable.

"Were you home this afternoon, Eva?" he asked, and she shook her head because she wasn't sure she could speak without tears rolling down her cheeks.

"Was Brady?"

"He was with his babysitter. Mrs. Daphne lives two doors down," she managed to say past the lump in her throat.

"Is that close to Slade McNeal's place?" he asked.

And odd question, but she'd answer whatever he asked if it meant getting him outside searching for Brady.

"Yes."

Detective Black and Officer Cunningham exchanged a look she couldn't read. One that excluded her, made her even more terrified than she already was.

"What's going on?"

"Captain McNeal's father was attacked today. His dog, Rio, was stolen. The person responsible is still on the loose."

"What does that have to do with Brady?" she asked, but she knew, the cold icy feeling in her heart making her shake.

"It's going to be okay." Detective Black walked

across the room and opened the front door. "I'm going to get Justice. Eva, if you want to get a photo of your son and an article of his clothing. Something that he wore today, preferably. I'll be back in a minute."

She ran into Brady's room, trying not to think about Slade's father, his missing K-9 partner. Trying not to think about how pale and quiet Brady had been when she'd picked him up from Mrs. Daphne's house.

He hadn't eaten much for dinner.

Maybe he'd just been sick. A stomach virus. Kids got those all the time.

She wanted to believe that accounted for his silence at the dinner table, his desire to go to bed early.

Check the window again, Momma. Did you check it?

The words seemed to echo in Brady's empty room.

She should have asked him why he was worried about the window lock. Should have pressed him about his day, asked just one more time if everything was okay.

If she had—

"Did you find something?" Detective Black walked into the room, a bloodhound padding along beside him. Orange vest and droopy ears, a wet nose and big, dark eyes. Brady would have loved to see him.

The thought burned behind Eva's eyes, and she ran to the closet, yanked out the T-shirt Brady had worn to school.

Blue today. Orange tomorrow!

"This is the shirt he wore today." She handed the detective Brady's T-shirt before she gave into temptation and pressed it to her face, inhaled her son's little-boy scent.

Please, God. Please.

"He asked me to check the window lock twice. He seemed quiet at dinner. I thought he might be getting sick, but maybe…" Her guilt spilled out, and she had to stop the words so that the tears didn't spill out, too.

"Your son's disappearance might not have anything to do with what happened at Slade's house."

"But you think that it does?"

"Do you have a recent photo?" He didn't respond to her comment, and she knew that he did.

She hadn't realized she could be any more petrified than she'd been when she'd walked into Brady's room and seen his open window.

She could be.

She *was.*

Cold air blew in, carrying a hint of rain or snow.

And, somewhere out in the darkness, Brady was scared and probably calling for her.

A tear dripped down her cheek.

"Eva, I need that photo," Detective Black said gently, and she ran from the room, ran into hers.

So close to Brady's.

She'd planned it that way when she'd decided which of the three bedrooms she'd take and which Brady would have.

So close, but she hadn't heard a sound until he'd cried for her.

She grabbed the framed school photo from her nightstand, pressed it to her chest.

"Got it?" Detective Black walked into the room with his bloodhound, and Eva didn't care that she'd left her waitressing uniform in a stack on a chair. She didn't care that a pile of college books and papers lay beside her bed. She didn't care about anything but handing him the photo and watching him walk out the door to find her son.

"This was taken a few months ago." She handed him the photo, and he studied it for a moment.

"Cute kid," he said with a small smile, and she nodded because she couldn't speak past the tears that clogged her throat.

The doorbell rang again. This time she didn't run to answer it. Didn't believe that somehow Brady would magically appear on the porch, tired and scared but with some explanation that would make sense. Maybe some story about sleepwalking or thinking that Mrs. Daphne's dog was outside whining for his attention.

She walked into the living room, her heart heavy and aching, her chest tight.

Captain Slade McNeal stood near the front door, his dark hair mussed, his face drawn and weary. "Eva, I'm sorry I couldn't be here sooner. I had to wait for my son's babysitter to arrive."

"It's okay." Her voice sounded hollow and old.

"Have you found any evidence, Cunningham?" Slade turned to the patrol officer.

"I checked the back window. It looks like someone popped the lock on it. I've already called for an evidence team."

"Good. Are you going to take Justice out to track Brady, Austin?"

"Yes. We'll start around back and work our way from there."

"I'll come with you." Eva pulled her old wool coat from the closet near the door. There was no way she could put Brady's life in someone else's hands. No way she could trust that anyone else would look as hard or as long as she would. He was her son, after all. Her responsibility.

"The best thing you can do for your son is stay here and answer the captain's questions. The more information you provide, the faster we can narrow down our search." Austin walked onto the porch, and she followed.

He might not want her to help with the search, but she had no intention of staying behind. Brady needed her, and she needed to be there for him. That was the way it had been from the moment he was born, the bond between them so strong that she'd thought that nothing would ever tear them apart.

Something had.

Some*one* had.

She clenched her fist.

Brady was okay. He had to be.

"I've called in Lee Calloway. I'll have him question the neighbors while I work with Cunningham and the evidence team." Slade stepped outside, and Eva walked down the porch stairs, letting him approach Detective Black. They could talk all they wanted. She was going to look for her son.

Please, God, just let him be okay. Please, help me find him.

Please.

She could not lose her son.

Wouldn't lose him.

If that meant searching alone while the police collected evidence and speculated on the who and why and how of Brady's kidnapping, so be it.

TWO

Justice whined impatiently as Austin followed Eva around the side of the house. She stood near the window, staring aimlessly into the backyard, her arms wrapped around her waist.

"You need to go back inside," he said.

"I need to find my son, Detective. He's my life."

"I know." Austin didn't have children yet, but he'd heard the same story dozens of times over his years in search and rescue. He knew the depth of fear and longing, the hope and despair that lived in a parent's heart when a child disappeared. "I'm going to help you do that, but you need to help me."

"By going inside and answering a thousand questions?" she asked, her eyes shimmering with tears. None fell. She looked young, but tough. Like someone who'd lived through trouble, and who expected to live through more.

"If that's what it takes to find Brady, then, yes."

"I can't go back inside."

"You have to, because the longer I have to stand here talking to you, the longer it's going to take me to get started on the search."

"I—"

"Go inside, Eva." He cut her off, crouched near Justice and held out Brady's shirt. "Ready, boy?"

Justice snuffled the fabric, then bent his long snout to the ground. He circled the area, bypassing Eva, who didn't seem at all interested in following orders.

"Do you think he can find Brady's scent?" she asked.

"Yes."

"Will it lead us to Brady?"

"Hopefully."

"What—"

"Justice is ready to track. I can't let him start until you're inside."

His words were like a splash of ice water in Eva's face.

Of course, he couldn't start the search while she stood there asking questions.

She blinked back hot tears, hating the weakness that made her want to beg and plead and cry. She was strong. She had to be, but she didn't feel strong. She felt weak and scared, and she wanted to hover around Austin until he promised that he'd bring Brady home to her.

She pivoted, willing to do anything to have Brady back.

"Eva," Detective Black called as she reached the corner of the house.

"Yes?" She stopped, but she didn't turn to face him. She didn't want him to see her despair.

"I'll do everything I can to bring Brady home to you."

She did turn then, wanting to thank him for the reassurance. The words died as she watched him hold Brady's little shirt out to the dog.

Justice huffed out a breath and barked.

"Seek," Detective Black commanded, and the bloodhound took off, his handler running along behind him. Across the backyard, into the neighbor's. Out onto the street beyond.

She lost sight of them there.

If she could have, she would have followed them, but she knew she had to go back. Do what she'd been told. Answer dozens of questions that might, if God were willing, bring her son home.

He certainly hadn't been willing to bring her parents' murderer to justice, but she had to believe that this time He'd answer her prayers.

Please, God. Please.

She walked around to the front of the house, skirting by several police officers who were standing on the front porch. Three police cars were parked on the curb, another one across the street. One in the driveway. Lots of people, and that had to be a good thing.

Didn't it?

She hoped so, because every minute that passed was a minute that Brady was alone with…

She cut the thought off. Didn't want to acknowledge what had been floating around in her head since Detective Black had mentioned the crime at Slade's house.

Had Brady seen something?

He shouldn't have. He wasn't allowed to play outside by himself, and Mrs. Daphne didn't like being outside in the cold. Arthritis, she always said, and who was Eva to say differently? At seventy, Mrs. Daphne deserved to stay inside if it was what she wanted. The rule was, Brady stayed inside with her. A tough one for him to want to follow. He was high energy and active, and he loved being outdoors.

Had he skirted the rule?

Snuck outside or convinced Mrs. Daphne to let him go?

Her house was close enough to Slade's for Brady to have had a clear view of it from the yard. But could he have seen enough to make him the target of a criminal?

She didn't know. Didn't even want to speculate. All she wanted was her son.

She walked back inside, tried to return the

smile that Slade offered. "Do you have some questions for me? Because if you don't—"

"I do. Officer Cunningham is working with the evidence team, and I'll be conducting the interview. This should only take a few minutes."

"All right." She sat on the edge of the couch, her body trembling and cold.

"Was Brady with Mrs. Daphne today?"

"Yes."

"What time did you pick him up?"

"Six."

"Did he mention anything unusual about his day? Anything that concerned you or him?"

"Nothing. He did seem…quiet." She knew where the conversation was heading, and she took a deep breath, tried to relax.

He narrowed his eyes. "You heard what happened at my house yesterday afternoon?"

"Yes. Detective Black told me."

"Then you know that my father was attacked and Rio was stolen. Do you think it's possible that Brady saw what happened?"

"He didn't mention it, but I guess anything is possible."

Slade jotted something in a notebook, asked another question and another.

Eva answered all of them as best she could. She couldn't collapse, couldn't let herself give in to the emotions that beat like bat wings in her stomach.

She wanted to, though. Almost wished she had someone to lean on. Someone who could put an arm around her shoulder and tell her everything would be all right. There was no one. She wasn't sure there ever had been.

The clock on the fireplace mantel ticked the time away. Five minutes. Ten. Fifteen.

Nearly an hour since Eva had realized Brady was gone.

An hour that he'd been missing. An hour that he'd been terrified, cold. Hungry, because he always was.

She wiped clammy hands on her pajama pants, swallowed down bile. "Are we almost done, Slade?"

"I just have a few more questions to ask."

"I've already answered dozens, and I've answered some of them more than once."

"We have to be thorough, Eva. It's the only way to get your son back."

"The only way to get my son back is to go out and look for him. That's what I'm going to do." She stood, her legs shaky. "Where's Detective Black?"

"Tracking Brady. If things go well, your son will be home before dawn."

"And if they don't?"

"I can't answer that, Eva. Sometimes kids are

returned home in an hour or two. Sometimes it takes longer."

She sucked in a breath. "And sometimes it doesn't happen at all?"

"I think you know the answer to that. I also think that you know we'll do everything we can to bring Brady home to you."

She'd wanted reassurance.

She'd gotten truth, instead.

She should be thankful for it but she just felt sick, her stomach heaving, stars dancing in front of her eyes. "I need some air."

She ran outside, letting cold air bathe her hot face.

"Is everything okay, Ms. Billows?" Officer Cunningham asked, stepping away from a group of officers he'd been talking to.

"Do you know where Detective Black is?" If Slade couldn't give her an exact location, maybe he could.

"He's organizing the search team."

"Where?"

"Headquarters are at the east entrance of the Lost Woods. We have a team setting up there. I'm sure Captain McNeal explained everything to you."

Eva nodded as if he had, but she'd been told nothing. Maybe Slade hadn't known. Maybe he just hadn't told her. The second seemed more likely than the first. He'd taken several phone calls during the interview. At some point, he must have been told that Detective Black was setting up at the Lost Woods.

He had chosen not to share the information.

It didn't surprise her. She'd learned all about police silence after her parents' deaths.

She walked back inside, grabbed her purse, slipped her feet into old sneakers.

"Where are you heading?" Slade asked.

"I told you that I was going to go look for my son."

"I can't recommend that."

"Can you stop me?" Because unless he had a legal reason to keep her at the house, she didn't plan on being there. Not for a minute longer.

He hesitated, then sighed. "You're not a suspect, and you've answered all my questions. As long as I can get in touch with you if I need to, I guess I can't keep you here."

"I have my cell phone." She jotted the number on a scrap of paper and handed it to him, trying hard not to look into his eyes. She respected Slade. He was a good man who'd always been a good neighbor, but if his son, Caleb, were the one missing, he wouldn't be sitting in his house answering questions while other people searched.

"Just be sure you don't get in the way of the search, Eva. If you do, it won't help Brady."

"I know. I just need to…be doing something." She grabbed Brady's coat from the closet, telling herself that she was bringing it to him. That she'd go to the Lost Woods and see him standing with the search team, cold but fine.

She jogged down the porch stairs and across the yard, unlocking the station wagon and sliding in behind the wheel. She slammed the door closed as several people called out to her. A few were neighbors. One was a stranger, a reporter maybe.

She didn't care.

All she cared about was Brady.

"Please, for once, just start!" she muttered as she shoved the key into the ignition. The starter clicked once, then again. Finally, the engine sputtered to life and she pulled away from the curb, glad for once for her father's advice. *Never park in the driveway or the garage, kid. If you do, it'll be too easy for the police to block in your vehicle and keep you from running.*

Yeah, Ernie had been overflowing with little tidbits of information. Especially when he'd been drinking.

A police cruiser pulled in behind her, lights on. No sirens, though. No doubt Slade had called in a tail. He'd probably call it an escort. Either way, Eva knew her rights, and she didn't stop or slow down. That was another thing Ernie had taught her.

He'd also taught her that people couldn't be

trusted. Not strangers, not friends and certainly not family. A good lesson that she'd forgotten once and would never forget again.

The road leading out of the neighborhood was nearly empty, the moon hanging low above distant trees. A quarter mile, and she was outside Sagebrush city limits, sparse trees and thick scrub lining the two-lane highway. She knew the way to the Lost Woods. There weren't many people in Sagebrush who didn't. The place was legend, the deep wilderness a siren's song that had called more than one explorer to his doom.

She shivered, flicking on the heater and grimacing as cold air blew out of the vent. The car was a junker, but it ran. Until she finished school and got a better-paying job, there was no way she could afford better. It didn't matter. She and Brady had what they needed and they had each other. She'd told herself that often over the years. She'd believed it, too. As much as she cringed when she thought about the mistake she'd made, the lies she'd bought into, the things she'd given away, she couldn't regret Brady.

A tear slipped down her cheek. The second of the night, and if she wasn't careful there would be more. She tightened her grip on the steering wheel, her fingernails digging into hard plastic as she turned onto the narrow road that led to the east entrance of the woods.

If Justice *had* tracked Brady to the woods, it meant he'd found the trail and been on it for nearly half a mile. Good news, but Eva didn't want to think about Brady wandering through the wilderness. Anything could happen in the thick shelter of the Lost Woods. Anything could be lost there and never found again.

She pulled in behind a line of police cars, search-and-rescue vehicles and TV-news vans. A crowd of people stood in the glow of several oversize spotlights, huddled around a long table, staring at something spread across its top. A tall broad-shouldered man gestured to the table and then to the entrance of the woods, his sweeping motion including stately pine trees crowded close and giant oaks that seemed to bar entrance to the forest's dark interior.

Detective Austin Black.

Exactly the man Eva wanted to see.

She grabbed Brady's coat and jumped out of the station wagon, ignoring the officer who was getting out of the patrol car behind her.

"Detective Black!" she called, pushing past a couple of news photographers.

"Come on over." He didn't look surprised to see her. Had probably been warned that she was on her way. Good, because she didn't want to waste more time arguing about whether or not she should be there.

She squeezed in between him and a dark-haired officer who held the leash of a border collie.

"What's going on?" she asked.

"Justice and I tracked your son to the entrance of the woods. We were able to follow the scent trail to a stream about a half mile in. We lost it there, but I think Justice can pick it up again. We'll have four teams working quadrants from here." Detective Black jabbed at a map of the Lost Woods, the cool leather of his jacket brushing her cheek. She caught a whiff of pine needles and soap and some indefinably masculine thing. It settled into the pit of her stomach, mixing with her fear and worry, the combination shivering through her blood, lodging in the base of her skull. It pounded there. The beginning of a migraine.

She took a deep breath, trying to ignore the stabbing pain and concentrate on the map.

"Do you really think he's in the woods?"

"It's not what I think that matters. It's what Justice's nose says, and it's saying your son went into the woods. I don't know yet whether or not he's come out."

"Is it possible that he ran from his kidnapper and came here on his own?" That would be so much easier to think about than Brady with someone who had beaten a man just a few hours ago.

"His kidnapper was still with him at the stream.

I found footprints on the bank. One child-size print. Three adult boot prints."

"There's more than one kidnapper?"

"I didn't say that. I just said there were multiple footprints." He turned his attention back to the team.

"We're going to split up from here. I'd like you to cover that section, Lee." He used a highlighter to mark a rectangle of forest, and the man beside him nodded. He marked two other sections, calling out names of people Eva didn't know, but who she had to trust to do everything they could to find her son.

"I'll take the last quadrant," he said, marking the spot. Acres of land. That's what he was talking about. Miles of wilderness they had to search, and Brady maybe somewhere in the middle of it.

"Any questions?" Austin asked.

No one on the search team seemed to have any. Eva did.

She wanted to know what the temperature was, wanted to know how long it would take for a little boy dressed in nothing but flannel pajamas to succumb to hypothermia. She wanted to know what kind of person would beat an elderly man, steal a dog, kidnap a child, and she wanted to know how likely it was that Brady was still ali—

No.

She already knew the answer to the last one. He *was* alive.

She could feel it in her gut. She backed away from the table and the map and the group, because she couldn't bear to look at that expanse of wilderness and picture her son lost somewhere in the middle of it. Something bumped into the back of her legs. Or maybe she bumped into it. Whatever the case, she nearly fell over.

"Careful." A warm hand wrapped around her wrist, and she looked straight into Detective Black's midnight-blue eyes. Thick black lashes, laugh lines fanning out from the corners. Handsome, hard-edged and someone she desperately wanted to believe in.

"I'm okay." She pulled away, looked down at the thing that she'd tripped over.

The *dog*.

Justice, with his tongue lolling and his dark eyes gleaming, his droopy face matched by his droopy ears. He looked sweet and a little silly, and Eva thought again that Brady would love to meet him.

She touched his head, feeling knobby bones beneath velvety fur. "Brady would love you."

"Hopefully they'll meet soon." Austin scratched the bloodhound behind his ears, crouched and held Brady's shirt in front of him. A *piece* of Brady's shirt.

His favorite blue one, cut into pieces.

She'd buy him another one when he got home. Maybe she'd buy him four, because the little savings that she'd managed to secret away didn't matter if he wasn't around when she spent it.

She swallowed hard as Austin put the square of fabric into a plastic bag, tucked it into a backpack and shoved a hardhat fitted with a searchlight onto his head.

"How long do you think it will take to find him?" she asked.

"I don't know, and it wouldn't be fair to you if I speculated. I'll be calling updates in to Captain McNeal, though. He should be here shortly." He gazed down at her. "Why don't you wait for him in your car so you don't get hounded by the press?"

"I—"

Austin issued a command to Justice and walked away, obviously not interested in a discussion.

That was fine.

Eva wasn't interested in one, either.

She followed him across the small clearing that narrowed onto a hiking path, buttoning her coat against the cold wind as they walked deeper into the blackness of the woods.

THREE

Eva didn't plan to give up. She was bound and determined to help find her son.

That much was obvious.

It was also obvious that having her wandering around in the Lost Woods could only lead to trouble. Dozens of hikers had been lost there over the years. Some had been recovered. Many hadn't.

Austin had been on plenty of search-and-rescue missions in the thousand-acre wilderness. He knew the area well, and even *he* got turned around on occasion.

"You need to go back to base camp," he barked over his shoulder, Justice tugging at the lead, anxious to be given his head.

Eva didn't reply.

Not a word.

Not even a hint that she'd heard.

He pulled Justice to a stop, aggravated, annoyed and frustrated.

"I'm searching for your son, Eva. You're slowing me down."

"I have his coat. It's cold tonight. He's going to need it." She held out a thick blue coat, her arm shaking, her voice steady.

"Thanks." He took it, tucked it into his backpack, not bothering to explain that he had plenty of blankets and knew how to warm someone with hypothermia.

"Do you think he's okay? It's freezing out here, and he's just a little guy."

"We're in the forties. That's well above freezing."

"You know what I mean, Detective."

"Austin." He urged Justice to seek again, not willing to stop for a conversation. Not wanting to spend any more time trying to assuage Eva's worry. She needed to go back and wait. It was as simple as that.

Unfortunately, forcing the issue and dragging her back would waste time they didn't have.

Forty-three degrees *was* cold. Especially for a kid who wasn't dressed for the weather.

"If he's still with his kidnapper, do you think that—"

"Eva, I don't have time for a question-and-answer game, okay? If you want to have that, then go back to the head of the trail. I'm sure Slade is there. He can answer every question you want to ask."

"I can't go back. Not when Brady is out here somewhere."

"You'll be helping him more if you go back. Do you understand that you're slowing me down?"

"Go as fast as you want. I can keep up."

"For how long?"

"As long as it takes."

"That could be hours. You know that, right?"

She didn't respond, and he glanced over his shoulder, irritated by her presence. She was a wrench in the works, a roadblock getting in the way of the smooth teamwork that he and Justice usually achieved without effort. "This is your son's life that we're talking about, Eva."

"I know," she said simply. No dramatics. No tears.

"Then you'll understand why it's better for me and Justice to do this alone."

"Let me ask you something, Austin. Do you have any idea how it feels to wake up in the middle of the night and realize that your child is missing?

"No," he responded honestly.

"Then you can't understand why I need to be here."

"You're wrong. I *can* understand. But finding the missing is what Justice and I are trained to do. We put everything we have into it every time. You can trust us with your son's life."

"I don't trust anyone. Especially not when it comes to Brady."

"This time, you don't have a choice."

"Sure I do. I trusted the police to find my parents' murderer. That hasn't happened. I trusted Brady's father to keep his promises. Look where that got me." She laughed, the sound achingly sad. "Now, I trust God and myself. That's it."

"I'm not anyone you've dealt with before, Eva. Maybe you should keep that in mind."

"What's that supposed to mean?"

"When I'm on search and rescue, every person I'm looking for is my family. I don't leave family behind. Not ever. As long as there's a chance of recovering Brady, I'll be out here searching for him."

"Who decides when there isn't a chance?" she asked quietly.

"Time." He shoved through thick foliage, holding back branches so they didn't slap her in the face.

"How much time?" Eva persisted.

"I don't know. Every situation is different."

"I can't go home without him." Her voice quivered, and Austin remembered the softness in her eyes when she'd held her son's photograph. The lone tear that had slid down her cheek. She was tough, but she was also a mother whose child was missing.

"Then let's both pray that you don't have to," he said, because he wouldn't promise that he'd find Brady. No matter how much he wanted to. He'd gone down that path before. It had ended in tragedy and heartache.

For a moment, Eva was silent.

Maybe she was waiting for the vows that Austin wouldn't make, hoping that he'd reassure her, tell her that finding Brady was a certainty.

"Thanks," she finally said. Nothing else. No begging or pleading for a guarantee.

"For what?"

"For not feeding me a bunch of lies about how certain you are that you'll find my son."

"You deserve the truth, and the truth is, I can't promise a good outcome, but I'm going to do everything that I can to make sure we have one. Come on. Let's pick up the pace."

He loosened his hold on the leash, allowing Justice more slack. The bloodhound leaped forward, his paws scrambling in the thick layer of fallen leaves and pine needles. They'd searched this area before, and Justice followed the scent trail easily, baying once and then taking off.

Austin ran behind him, his feet pounding on packed earth and slippery leaves. No thought of Eva and whether or not she could keep up, just focusing on the feel of the lead in his hand, the tug of Justice's muscular body, the tension that surrounded both of them.

Justice stopped at a small creek, sniffing the ground and moving back and forth across the creek bed. He stopped at a small flag, his tail wagging slightly as he acknowledged the area that they'd searched so intently, the prints that Austin had cast and photographed.

"Seek," Austin urged, and Justice bent his nose to the ground again, his ears dragging along the wet creek bank.

Nothing.

Another ten minutes. Fifteen.

He pulled Justice up with a quick command, bent to study a small footprint pressed into the earth. Five toes. A little heel.

A little boy walking with his kidnapper or running from him?

Eva crouched beside him, her pants dragging in the mud, her sneakers caked with it. "His feet must be so cold."

"Kids are pretty hardy." He tried not to think about the children who hadn't been. The lifeless bodies he'd found on riverbanks and in deep forests. Tried not to remember little Anna Lynn. Missing for four days before Austin had finally been able to bring her back to her parents. She'd been the daughter of one of his closest friends.

The search hadn't ended the way he'd wanted it to.

Never again.

That's what he'd told himself. No more emotional involvement. No more allowing himself to be so personally invested. But how could he not be when a little kid was lost, scared and alone?

He shoved the thoughts away and stood. "He headed downhill from here. We picked up the trail at a creek there. Come on."

He led the way down the steep hill, Justice panting behind him. He gave the bloodhound a minute to lap water from the cool creek, then pulled the shirt from his pack again.

"Seek!" he commanded.

Justice raised his head, sniffing the air.

"Seek!" Austin encouraged, and Justice ran to the edge of the creek, snuffled at the ground.

Nothing.

"Do you—"

"How about we just let him work?" Austin cut Eva off. He needed to focus. Needed to keep moving. Time was ticking by. Brady was still missing. As much as Austin had tried to play it cool with Eva, he knew how quickly a child could become hypothermic. Especially a wet child. Brady had walked through two creeks and there was a hint of moisture in the cold air. The clouds might open at any moment, pouring down rain or ice.

Please, Lord, help us find him before then.

He let Justice work the area around the creek for fifteen minutes, then led him from the water, Eva pressing in so close that he could hear her soft breath, feel the warmth of her body through layers of cloth. She had a presence about her, and even in silence, she was difficult to ignore.

In the distance a dog barked, and Justice cocked his head to the side, then bent it to the ground again. Still nothing.

Brady and his captor might have come this way a couple of hours ago, the scent trail diluted by time and forest life, but giving up wasn't an option. Not now. Not an hour from now. Until Brady was home, Austin would keep searching.

Slow. That's the way they were moving, circling one area after another as Justice nosed the ground. Eva didn't say another word. No questions. No idle chatter. She just followed along, stayed out of the way, and let Austin and his bloodhound do their job. She wanted to run, though. Race past them both screaming Brady's name. Hoping he would answer.

Dim light filtered through the tree canopy, the first rays of the rising sun breaking through the forest's gloom. The area felt empty, Justice's soft huffs seeming to fade into the expanse of wilderness that surrounded them. They moved up a steep ridge, crisscrossing the leaf-strewn ground as Justice searched for the trail. He paused, nose to the air, body taut. One quick bark and he strained against the leash, his powerful body plowing through thick foliage.

"Do you think he's found Brady?" Eva panted as she shoved through a tangle of tree branches. Her hair snagged on a twig, and she yanked away, her eyes tearing from pain, her pulse humming with hope and fear.

"He's found the scent again. How far we'll be able to track it is hard to say." Austin's answer was brief, his breathing unlabored. He didn't even look winded, his long legs eating up the ground as he followed Justice.

"I can't believe that Brady walked this far."

And she didn't want to picture all the ways that he might have gotten there if he *hadn't* walked. Carried? Dragged?

"I've tracked kids that have walked farther." Another brief answer. Fine. If Austin still wanted silence, she'd give it to him.

She didn't speak again as they crested the ridge and ran down the other side. Justice stopped at the bottom, and Eva's heart stopped with him. If he lost the trail, would he find it again?

Justice barked, his body seeming to vibrate with energy as he strained against the leash. They were heading into hill country, the woods deepening, the feeling of being cut off from time and place growing. They ran along the edge of a steep ravine, following a game trail that wound its way through the forest. No sign of anyone or anything, but Eva was sure they were being watched. Unseen eyes staring out of the shadowy woods and tracking their movements.

A branch snapped to their right, and Austin stopped, pulling Justice up short and issuing a sharp command for the dog to cease. His dark hair gleamed in the early-morning sunlight, his hard face shadowed with the beginnings of a beard. If Eva had been alone in the woods and seen him, she'd have walked the other way.

He gestured her over, pressing his finger to his lips as she moved in close.

Another branch snapped and Eva tensed, sure that someone would step out of the woods.

Silence fell. Thick. Heavy. Expectant.

Austin pulled back his jacket, his hand falling to the gun belt at his waist, his icy gaze scanning the forest. Justice stood beside him, hackles raised, body stiff. What did he sense? A bear? A deer? A person?

Several minutes passed and Justice relaxed, settling onto his haunches, his floppy ears whipping as he shook his sturdy body.

Gone. Whatever had been in the trees, but Eva still felt the threat, still wondered what or who had been watching.

"Let's go," Austin said, issuing a command for Justice to seek. The dog jumped up, nose to the ground, energy pouring through his body. Seconds later he barked, straining against the leash as he led them up a steep incline.

They ran up another hill, plunged down it again. Wove their way through trees and up to a cliff that overlooked the forest, following a path that seemed disjointed and erratic. A trail laid by a frantic, scared little boy?

Dear God, she hoped so.

She wanted to crest the next rise, round the next tree, see Brady standing there waiting for her.

She tripped, slid a few feet forward on her hands and knees, the earth near the cliff's edge crumbling and falling away. A thirty-foot drop, at least. Her heart jumped, and she scooted back.

"Careful." Austin appeared at her side, tugged her upright, his hands on her waist. There. Gone. So quickly she should barely have felt them. She did, though, his touch burning deep, reminding her of things better forgotten. Her cheeks heated, but there wasn't time to think about it or to care.

Justice scrambled up a steep hill, his paws churning up leaves and dirt. Austin followed easily, grabbing tree branches and fists full of foliage as he fought his way to the top. Eva slipped and slid behind them.

Austin grabbed her hand as she neared the top,

tugging her onto a ridge that overlooked the forest. A mountain of foliage shot up to the right. To the left, the ground fell away. A hundred feet below the trees huddled close, their winter-bare branches revealing glimpses of the forest floor.

Not a safe place for a seven-year-old boy, and Eva's heart jolted with panic.

"What if he fell?" she whispered, the words barely carrying past the lump in her throat.

"He didn't. Justice is still locked on to his scent. Come on." Austin let the dog pull ahead again, and they skimmed the edge of the cliff, the slippery leaves and loose dirt slowing their progress.

Eva glanced into the abyss to the left, her head swimming as she imagined Brady falling head over heels.

Please, God. Let him be okay.

A fat branch slapped her cheek, the stinging pain barely registering past the hollow thud of her fear. She felt sick with it, her stomach and chest tight, her breathing labored. Everything she loved was wrapped up in Brady.

Austin stopped short and she ran into his back, her feet slipping on thick leaves as she tried to catch her balance.

He snagged her arm, pulling her forward as he crouched near Justice. The dog whined excitedly, his deep bark breaking the morning stillness.

"Release," Austin said, and Justice backed

away, dropping down beneath a thick-trunked oak and panting heavily.

"Look at this." Austin pointed to something half-hidden by leaves and dirt. At first Eva couldn't make out what it was. White and gray and brown fuzz covered by forest debris. A splash of bright blue.

"Is it an animal?" she asked, leaning closer, the truth suddenly right there in front of her face. Blue plastic eyes, a shiny black nose, white fluffy face.

"A *stuffed* animal," he responded.

"Snowflake! Brady must have brought it with him." She reached for it, and he captured her hand, gently pulling it back.

"It's evidence, Eva. We don't want it contaminated." He lifted the stuffed dog with a gloved hand, tucked it into a plastic bag he pulled from his pack.

"He was here! Brady was here!" She stood, whirling around, frantically searching for some other sign that her son was close.

"Yeah. And it looks like he was alone this time. Look." Austin pointed to a small footprint in the dusty earth. Bare. Every toe clearly defined. Another was just a few inches away. No sign of boot prints like the ones at the creek.

That was good.

Right?

"He must be terrified." She wanted to cry but couldn't let the tears come.

"I'm going to radio in and get the other search teams to the area. We'll do better consolidating our efforts. Drink this while I get people organized." He handed her an energy drink, poured water into a small dish for Justice.

Maybe Eva should have opened her energy drink, drank it up as quickly as Justice lapped up his water. But she felt too sick, her head throbbing endlessly, her stomach churning. Worry beat a rapid pulse through her blood, and she wanted to sit down and close her eyes. Open them again and find herself back in bed, Brady safe in the room beside hers.

"We're set." Austin clipped his radio into place, frowned at Eva's still-full bottle. "You're not going to do Brady any good if you're dehydrated and exhausted."

He took the bottle from her hand, opened it and handed it back to her, his fingers warm and callused. There was something comforting about that. Something nice and a little too wonderful about the way it felt to look into his face, see his concern and his determination.

She swallowed a few large gulps of the energy drink. Took two more sips for good measure, and then recapped the lid.

"Happy?" she asked, feeling vulnerable beneath his steady scrutiny.

"I'd be happier if you let me call someone to escort you out of the woods, but since I don't want to waste time arguing, I think it's best if I just say yes." He tucked Justice's empty bowl into his pack, took the energy drink and did the same. "Seek!"

They were off again, and Eva had to swallow hard to keep the drink from coming back up. Her stomach heaved, but Justice was on the trail, lunging against his collar and leash, his orange vest bright in the watery dawn light.

He ran like the best think in the world lay at the end of the scent trail he was following, ran like he couldn't wait to be united with the boy that he was seeking. Ran like it mattered, and Eva thought that if she ever gave in to Brady's begging for a puppy, she'd get him a bloodhound. Maybe Austin could give them some tips on how to train a dog. Maybe...

She shoved the thought away.

Thinking ahead, planning for Brady's return... that was one thing. Planning to include Austin in their lives after Brady was found, that was something she wouldn't allow herself to do.

Sweat trickled down her face as they raced past trees and headed up a small hill. Sunlight speckled the ground with gold and warmed the winter chill, the world a blur of gold and green and brown, the only sound Justice's frantic barks and Eva's panting breath.

Something snapped behind her, the sound so loud and startling she turned, caught a glimpse of a dark figure deep in the woods. There. Gone. There again. Moving away from them, but somehow sinister in the forest stillness.

"You okay?" Austin asked, and she realized she'd stopped, was searching the trees.

"I saw someone." She pointed to the area where the figure had disappeared.

"Probably search and rescue."

"He wasn't wearing an orange vest like yours, and he didn't have a dog."

An explosion ripped through the morning quiet. One short sharp report and then another.

A gun!

Austin shouted something, and she was falling, colors swirling around her as she landed hard on the thick pine carpet.

FOUR

"Stay down," Austin whispered, his breath brushing her ear. Justice nudged her cheek but she didn't move, barely even jumped as another shot rang out.

Her heart thundered, her body braced for the bullet's impact. When it didn't come, she tried to get up and find cover, but Austin's body pressed over hers, holding her still.

"They're not shooting at us, but let's make sure we don't get caught in the crossfire."

"Brady—" She tried to move, but he was a solid wall of muscle, and she couldn't budge him.

"Dying isn't going to help your son, Eva."

"What if they're shooting at him?"

He was speaking into his radio and didn't respond.

She didn't think he would have, anyway. Whatever was happening, it was out of either of their control. Another shot rang out, and she flinched, her body screaming for her to get up, find Brady and make sure he was safe.

Something crashed in the underbrush to their right, and Eva turned her head, saw the gun in Austin's hand.

"Stay here." He left her lying on cold, hard earth, her heart pounding frantically, the thick coppery taste of fear in her mouth.

She lifted her head, watching as he moved away. Crouched low. Silent. If she hadn't been looking at him, she wouldn't have known he was there. Leaves rustled in a thicket a hundred yards away, and he froze. Eva froze, too, her muscles taut with fear.

"Police. Come out with your hands where I can see them," he commanded. More rustling. A soft sigh that might have been a moan. A woman stumbled from the thick tangle of overgrowth, blood streaming down her face. She fell to her knees. Managed to stand up again. Confused. Dazed. Not dangerous. That's what Eva thought, and Austin must have thought the same. He holstered his gun.

"Ma'am, are you okay?" Austin asked, moving toward her.

"What's going on? Where am I?" she replied, her gaze darting from Austin to Justice and then settling on Eva.

"The Lost Woods. You're hurt, and you need

to lie down." Eva took her arm, tried to help her to the ground.

"What happened?" She touched her head, frowning at her blood-tinged fingers.

"I was hoping you could tell us." Austin pulled off his jacket, dropped it onto the woman's shoulders, his gaze scanning the forest. Danger still lurked there, but Justice lay docile in the shadows of a large oak, his big head resting on his paws.

"I...don't remember. I think..." Her gaze dropped to his gun holster, her eyes widening. "No!"

"Ma'am, I'm with the Sagebrush Police Department. Just relax, okay?" Austin put a hand on her shoulder, but she shrugged away, her eyes wild.

"Everything is going to be fine. I'm going to call for a rescue crew to come and transport you out of the forest."

"No!" she said again, whirling away, Austin's coat dropping to the ground as she plunged back into the thicket.

Austin started after her, heard the snap of branches and Justice's quiet bark. Not danger, but someone was coming. He turned, stepping in front of Eva just in case.

"What—"

He put his hand up, cutting off her words as he caught sight of an orange vest. Search and rescue. Hopefully, a police officer. Justice was on Brady's scent, and Austin didn't want to stop the search to chase after the injured woman or to find the person who had been firing shots at her.

"Hey! Austin! I heard gunfire and your call for backup. Is everything okay?" Detective Lee Calloway called out as he approached with his border collie, Kip. A fellow member of the Special Operations K-9 Unit, Lee had been a good friend and coworker for years. His dog, Kip, specialized in cadaver detection. Hopefully, Kip wouldn't have to put those skills to use in their search for Brady.

"We're fine, but there's an injured woman heading west. She may know who the shooter was."

"How bad are the injuries?"

"It was hard to tell. She had a head wound, and she seemed confused. Could be a concussion or a fractured skull."

"You want me to go after her or the missing boy?" Lee asked.

"Justice already has Brady's scent. Go after Jane Doe. And watch your back while you're at it. Someone is wandering around firing shots."

"Will do. You have a description of the woman for me?"

"Aside from the bleeding head wound?"

"Aside from that." Lee smiled, but his eyes were shadowed. Yesterday had been long for the entire team. The discovery of Slade's injured father and the realization that Rio had been taken had hit the unit hard.

"Long blond hair. About five-five. Slim build."

"Got it. I'll radio in when I find her."

After Lee headed west with Kip, Austin shrugged into his coat and backpack. Eva hovered a few feet away, her skin pale, her arms hugging her waist.

He didn't ask if she was ready.

He knew she would be. Even if she wasn't, she wouldn't admit it.

"Come on, boy," he urged, and Justice lumbered to his feet. "Seek!"

Justice took off, barking wildly.

Close.

They were close.

Austin felt it in the tension on the lead, the way Justice's muscles pulled taut. The bloodhound wanted to get to the end of the trail, wanted to find the person they were seeking, wanted it more than he wanted to sleep or eat or play. That's what made him a great search-and-rescue dog, his prey drive completely refocused into a stunning display of canine determination.

They crested one more rise, plunged down into a ravine, the ground slick with mud and dead leaves. Justice bayed once and again, frantically clawing at the ground in an effort to move more quickly.

A dozen yards ahead, a rocky outcrop sheltered

a small pool of stagnant water. Beyond that, Austin could make out thick foliage partially hiding what looked like the opening of a cave. Six feet high and maybe four feet wide, it was the perfect hiding place for a scared little boy. His heart lurched, and he unhooked Justice. Let him race ahead, his frantic alerts ringing through the cool dawn.

"Is that a cave? He's there, isn't he? Brady! Brady!" Eva ran toward the cave, and Austin snagged the back of her coat, pulling her up short.

"Wait here while I check things out."

"Check what out? He's there. Justice is going crazy trying to tell us that."

"I know, but I need to go in first. We heard gunfire earlier, and I don't want you in the middle of more of it," he said.

"He's in there. I know he is." She tried to twist away, but he kept hold of her coat.

"We don't know—"

"He's there." She looked into his eyes, and he saw hope in the depth of her gaze. Saw it in her face.

He wanted to believe that it was justified, but there was no telling what he'd find in the cave. As much as Austin wanted to think they were running toward a live rescue, things might not turn out that way. He didn't want Eva to find her son's lifeless body. Didn't want her to see what he'd seen too many times.

Maybe she saw that in *his* face.

She stilled, her green eyes staring into his, her long gold lashes sweeping her cheek and brow. She had eyes like her son's. He felt the weight of the picture that he'd tucked into his coat pocket. Felt the weight of her dreams and hopes piled on his shoulders.

"You think he might be dead," she rasped, and he couldn't deny it.

"Wait here," he said again, letting go of her coat and running toward the cave.

Thick muck sucked at his boots and splashed up his pant legs, the stagnant pool of water shallow and brown. Eva splashed through it behind him. Obviously unwilling to listen to his request.

He reached the cave a few steps ahead of her, ducked down and moved into dank blackness, following the sound of Justice's fading barks. A few large rocks butted against the side of the cave, and he skirted around them. From there, the opening narrowed until Austin's shoulders brushed the walls. Even crouched, his head touched the ceiling. He maneuvered sideways for several minutes, but short of shrinking down to child-size there was no way he could go farther.

"What's going on? Why are we stopping?" Eva

pressed in as if she wanted to shove him out of the way and hunt for Brady herself.

"It's too narrow. Going farther wouldn't be safe."

"I'm smaller than you. Let me go."

"We'll both have to back out first. No way can you squeeze past me."

"Okay." She backed up and he followed, his headlamp flashing on dark gray rock and moist brown earth. The cave went deeper than he'd expected, curving to the left, whatever lay behind the curve hidden in darkness.

Justice's long howl echoed against the walls, bouncing through the darkness, and Austin snagged Eva's hand. "Hold on! Justice is alerting. He's found something. Try calling your son."

"Brady? It's Mom. Are you in there?" Eva called past the lump of terror and hope in her throat. What if he *was* there, but couldn't answer? What if he was injured or…

"Momma?" The word was faint, but she heard it. Wanted to climb straight through Austin to follow the sound.

"Yes. It's me. I have Snowflake, too. I found him out in the woods while I was looking for you. Come on out, and we can all go home together." She tried to keep her voice steady, but she was so relieved, so thankful, her body felt weak with it.

"I can't." He was crying. She could hear the

tears in his voice, and if the walls hadn't been pressing so tight, if Austin hadn't been wedged so firmly into the opening, she would have gone to her son.

"Ask him if he's stuck, and ask him if there's a dog with him," Austin urged.

"Are you stuck, sweetie?"

"I'm lost. I got inside here, but I can't get out. It's too dark."

"Is there a dog with you, Brady?"

"Yes, but I didn't pet him."

"Those are the rules for normal times, but for today, you can pet the dog. He's special. Like Captain Slade's dog."

"Are you hurt, Brady? Can you walk?" Austin called out.

"Momma, are you still there? Who's that with you?" The fear in his voice was unmistakable, and her heart ached for everything he'd been through, her arms aching to pull him close, let him know that he was finally safe.

"A police detective. He and his dog have been helping me find you. Are you hurt?"

"No, and I can walk, too. And I petted the dog. He's soft…and he licked my face."

"His name is Justice," Austin said. "Do you feel the harness on his back?"

"Yes."

"If you hold on to that, Justice will lead you all the way out of the cave."

"Really?"

"Absolutely. Are you holding on?"

"Yes."

"Justice, come!" Austin ordered, and then nudged Eva. "Let's head out where there's more room to maneuver."

"But—"

"Justice found your son, Eva. Are you really not going to trust him to lead him out of the cave?" he asked as his radio crackled.

No. She wasn't going to trust him. Not if she had a choice. Trust was something given and then broken. She'd found that out one too many times. She backed up, anyway because the last thing she wanted was for all of them to get stuck in the cave because she'd succumbed to fear.

Austin's voice rumbled into the darkness as he called in their coordinates and asked for a rescue unit. Eva tried to let his words comfort her. If he was calling for transportation, he must believe that Brady and Justice would make their way out.

Sunlight speckled the dirt floor near her feet, and she stopped, cold, crisp air swirling around her ankles. She pressed a hand to Austin's back, stopping him before they collided. Firm muscle contracted beneath her palm, and she pulled her hand away, her heart thumping painfully.

Brady. He was all that mattered, and he hadn't appeared yet. Hadn't called out again.

"Brady?" she called, but he didn't answer. "What if—"

"He's coming." Austin pulled off his pack, rifled through it and took out a thermal blanket.

"I don't hear him or Justice."

"Justice already found what he was looking for. He's done alerting, and Brady probably couldn't hear you calling. The cave is a lot deeper than I anticipated." He sighed. "I'm glad you were with me. I don't know if your son would have come out otherwise."

His words took her by surprise. She'd thought him to be a little arrogant, a lot bossy. Not the kind of guy who would admit that he'd been wrong. Not the kind who she would have expected to give other people credit.

Then again, she'd never been the best judge of character. She certainly hadn't been when it came to Rick.

"Things always work out the way they're supposed to." Her mother used to say that to Eva. It had taken a lot of years for her to believe it.

"True, and this time, they worked out the way that we both wanted them to." He smiled, and it transformed his face, made him approachable in the easy charming way that would have appealed to her if she ever allowed any man to do that.

"Momma? Where are you?" Brady called, his voice muffled and distant.

Her heart jerked, the need to go to him so strong that she took a step deeper into the cave, peered into its shadowy depths.

"I'm right here, buddy. Are you still with Justice?"

"Yes, but it's dark, and I'm cold. I want to go home."

"Just keep walking, then. You'll be out of there before you know it," she called, hoping the words would comfort him.

"Use this. Brady might be able to see the light once he gets closer." Austin handed her his head-lamp, and she shone it into the cave. The light bounced off gray walls and brown floors. She wanted it to bounce off Brady's pale blond hair and freckled face.

She watched the narrow opening, her head pounding in time with her frantic heart. Finally, something moved in the darkness, a shifting of shadows that drew closer and closer, until the shadows had color and shape and form and Brady was in her arms. Clutching him close, she felt him shivering, his skin cold to the touch.

"You're freezing." Eva took off her coat and wrapped him in it, alarmed at his paleness. Scratches and dried blood scored his cheek and arms, and his feet were so caked with mud that she could barely see his toes. His pajama bottoms were torn at both knees, the skin peeking from beneath the fabric raw and bleeding.

"That's because I was cold all night. I was shaking I was so cold."

"Let's warm you up, okay?" She wrapped her arms around him, rubbing his back and trying to will some of her warmth into his cold little body.

"How are you doing, sport?" Austin wrapped the blanket around both of them, then crouched close, Justice panting contentedly near his feet.

"Okay. Are you the police?" Brady's eyes were wide, his teeth chattering, his lips so pale they faded into his skin.

"Yes. I'm Detective Austin Black. You already met my partner, Justice."

"He's a cool dog. I always wanted a dog, but Momma says that we're too busy to have one."

"It's not fair to have a dog if you don't have time," Austin responded diplomatically as he tucked the edges of the blanket around Brady's head.

"If I had a dog, those bad men would have stayed away from me."

"What bad men?" Austin pulled a juice box from his pack, popped a straw into it and handed it to Brady.

"They're not nice. They beat mean old Mr. McNeal and they took Rio."

"You saw the man who did that?" Eva asked, taking the untouched juice box from his hand and looking into his face. His lip trembled, his eyes swimming with tears.

"Yes," he whispered, looking away, obviously ashamed of something.

"How? You can't see Captain McNeal's house from Mrs. Daphne's."

"I walked Fluffy. Mrs. Daphne said that I could, because I was bored and I didn't want to watch stupid old TV anymore," he wailed.

Despite herself, Eva couldn't be upset. She couldn't even bring herself to remind him of the rule that he'd broken. Not yet. That would come when he was warm and clean and safe again.

"We'll talk about that later."

"How many men did you see, Brady?"

"Two. The man with the brown hair and the man with the red hair. The man with the red hair is meanest. He hit me right here, because I started crying when he brought me to the woods." Brady touched his cheek, tears spilling down his face. "He hit Mr. McNeal, too. With a brick. I even saw him do it. Then he pushed Rio right into a van and saw me."

"It's okay, buddy." Eva pressed his head to her shoulder.

"What happened next, sport?" Austin asked gently.

"The man with the red hair yelled for the other man to get me. Me and Fluffy ran really fast, though, and he didn't catch us."

"Why didn't you tell me about this, Brady? We could have called the police and made sure you were safe." Eva brushed Brady's hair from his forehead and looked into his denim-blue eyes. Rick's eyes, but so much softer and sweeter than his had been.

"Because you told me not ever to go walking by myself, and I didn't want to get into trouble." He started crying in earnest, his face scrunched up and so full of misery that Eva's heart broke.

"It's okay." She patted his back, and met Austin's eyes, anxious to get her shivering, sobbing son out of the cave and to safety. "How long until the rescue team arrives?"

"Ten or fifteen minutes. It might be best if we bring him out into the sun while we wait. He's hypothermic, and the sooner we get him warmed up, the better." He hooked Justice to his lead. "Ready to get out of here, Brady?"

"Yes." Brady didn't even lift his head. Ex-

hausted, bruised and terrified, but he was alive.
That was all that mattered.

Thank You, God.

Thank You, thank You, thank You.

Dawn peeked through the thick trees and dappled the ground with yellow-gold light as they walked out of the cave. Eva hadn't noticed the beauty of the forest while they were searching for Brady. Now she couldn't stop noticing. The tall pines stretching toward the blue sky. The red-brown earth beneath their feet. The soft sound of birds greeting the day.

Justice growled deep in his throat, the fur on his scruff standing on end, his nose pointed toward the rise above the cave.

"Go back into the cave," Austin shouted.

She didn't ask why. Didn't stop to think about who might be coming. She ran, feet slipping on slick ground, Brady in her arms, all the beauty of the morning fading into cold, stark terror.

FIVE

She set Brady down at the mouth of the cave, shielding him with her body as she shooed him away from the opening.

"Are they back, Momma? Are the bad men back?" Brady cried, his eyes wide in his stark white face.

"I don't—"

A shot rang out, the sound reverberating through the cave.

Close.

Too close.

"Let's go farther in, buddy." She nudged Brady in front of her, urging him deeper into the cave until the walls narrowed and Eva couldn't move forward any farther. She could hear nothing but her heartbeat and the soft rasping of Brady's breath. If Brady's bad men were following, they'd have easy targets, cave walls to either side, no room for Eva to move forward. Brady could, though.

"I want you to do what you did before, Brady.

Run deeper into the cave, okay? Not too far. Keep your hand on the wall and count twenty steps. As soon as you're done, turn right around this way so you know how to get out."

"No, Momma!"

"Yes. I'll have the detective send Justice in for you as soon as it's safe." She gave him a gentle shove, listening as his feet padded in the darkness. She counted his steps. Only ten, but she didn't want to call for him to keep going. She didn't want him any farther away than he needed to be.

She eased back the way she'd come, silently picking her way through the darkness, her hand sliding along the rough rock wall. She didn't know where Austin had gone, didn't know if the gunshot she'd heard had been from his gun or someone else's. The thought of him crumbling to the ground, blood flowing from a bullet wound, made her stomach ache and her pulse pound harder. He and Justice had saved Brady's life. Without them, her son would still be lost and shivering in the cave.

She shuddered at the thought, stepping out into the coolness of the cave's mouth. Thick foliage blocked her view of the shallow pool beyond it, but the morning had gone silent as death. Not a bird singing. No small animals rustling in the woods. Nothing, and that petrified her almost as much as the gunshot had. She searched the ground, grabbing a fist-size rock and creeping to the cave entrance. She peered through the overgrowth of shrubs and weeds, searching the landscape beyond.

Nothing.

No one.

Wait!

Her heart jumped as something moved in the forest. A man. Narrow build. Slim shoulders. Tall and thin, his red hair gleaming in the morning sun.

One of Brady's bad men. Where was the other?

And where were Austin and Justice?

She clutched the rock as the red-haired man made his descent. He glanced to his left and called to someone. Another man, picking his way into the ravine from the opposite slope. The only way out of the cave and into the woods was a straight path through the two of them.

The red-haired man stumbled the last few feet into the muck and dead leaves, his mud-brown eyes seeming to burn straight into Eva's.

She stumbled back and pressed close to the side wall of the cave. She didn't stand a chance against a bullet, but as long as Brady stayed deep in the cave, he'd be fine.

Please, God, let him be fine.

"Momma? Are they gone?" Brady called out,

his words bouncing off the granite walls and ringing through the unnatural silence.

That was all it took.

An explosion of sound, and a bullet whizzed past Eva's head, slammed into the cave wall, bits of granite showering her hair and face. She dove to the ground, scrambling away on her hands and knees, screaming for Brady to stay where he was.

Someone shouted, but Eva didn't hear the words past the echoing sound of gunfire.

Austin shouted another warning as he stepped from behind an outcrop of rocks and fired. His first shot hit home, dropping the redheaded perp who was closest to the cave. The other man retreated, racing back up the ravine and dodging behind a thick oak. Austin fired again, his bullet slamming into the tree's trunk. No way could he chase the man through the forest while Eva and Brady were alone in the cave. He called for backup and warned the approaching rescue team of the presence of the armed man as he ran to the cave.

He'd seen Eva behind the foliage, her pale face peering out, and he'd wanted to shout for her to take cover. He hadn't wanted to warn his targets, though. He hoped that he'd made the right choice. Hoped that she wasn't lying in a pool of blood on the other side of the winter-dry brush.

He paused at the fallen man's side, checked for

a pulse, knowing that he wouldn't find one. He'd done what he had to, but there was no joy in it.

"Is he dead?" Eva peered out of from the cave entrance, her hair a tangled mess around her shoulders, her eyes dull and tired.

"Yes." He shifted to block her view. "Are you and Brady okay?"

"Yes." An engine rumbled in the distance, and she glanced up the slope. "I guess that's our ride out of here. I'll tell Brady he can come out of hiding."

"Keep him in the cave, okay? I don't think it would be good for him to see this."

She glanced at the body, nodded and slipped back into the cave.

Austin patted the deceased's pockets, searching for ID. Nothing. They'd have to ID him by fingerprints or dental records.

He walked into the cave and unleashed Justice.

"Stay," he commanded, and the bloodhound dropped onto his haunches, his tongue lolling out, what looked like a contented smile on his hangdog face. He'd found the prize, discovered the missing, and he'd probably spend the rest of the day lying on the couch back at Austin's place.

"Can I pet your dog, Mr. Detective?" Brady asked as he walked from the deepest part of the cave, his white-blond hair dirty and spiking up around his head, the scratches on his face and arms livid. He'd lost his blanket and Eva's coat somewhere and shook violently. Austin pulled out another blanket and tucked it around his shoulders, concerned with his pallid complexion, his colorless lips, the vague look in his bright blue eyes.

"If it's okay with your mom." Austin glanced at Eva, who was clutching Brady's shoulder as if she were afraid that letting go would mean losing him again.

She nodded, and Austin called Justice to Brady's side.

"You can pet him, but only if you call me Austin and stay in the cave until I come tell you it's okay to come out. You also have to stay wrapped up real tight in this blanket, okay?"

"Okay."

Austin waited while Brady settled in beside Justice, smiling a little as the boy wrapped his arms around the dog's solid back and pulled the blanket over both of them. He'd soak in some of Justice's warmth. A good thing while they waited for rescue.

"I'll be right back." Austin stepped out of the cave and into the cold, sunny day. A few clouds edged across the horizon, the hint of moisture he'd felt earlier coalescing into a brewing storm.

The sound of approaching vehicles grew louder as he covered the perp's face with the blanket, said a silent prayer for the family of the man. The deceased might have chosen a dark path, but his family would still mourn his loss.

A four-wheeler roared into view, splashing through the small pool and stopping a few feet from the cave. A dark-haired woman jumped off. Austin knew her. Laurel Stanley worked as an emergency-room nurse and volunteered with San Antonio Search and Rescue. They'd dated a few times, but they both had busy lives and lived in cities they loved. Neither planned to move, and that, as much as anything, had kept the relationship from blooming.

"Hey, Austin! You've found the boy?"

"In the cave. Hypothermic. Shaky, but conscious."

"The sooner we get him out of here, the better, then." She hurried into the cave as a four-wheeler driven by a uniformed police officer arrived. Austin briefed him quickly, watching as he took off again, heading in the direction that the second perp had disappeared. More than likely, the guy was long gone by now, but they'd keep looking, keep hunting until he was in custody.

Two more four-wheelers roared toward Austin, the forest alive with sound and movement. The teams would need to take photos, collect evidence. Protocol always dictated, but when it came to lethal force, it was even more important that it be followed precisely.

He walked to the mouth of the cave, stepping back as Eva carried Brady out, Laurel right behind them.

"I'm transporting now, Austin. We'll bring them to Sagebrush General. I've already called ahead to let them know we're coming," she said.

"I'll make sure we have a man there." He wanted twenty-four-hour protection for Brady until they had the second perp in custody. Whatever Brady had witnessed, whoever he'd seen, it had been enough to put him in the sights of some very dangerous men.

"Thanks for everything, Austin," Eva said as she climbed onto the four-wheeler, Brady leaning against her shoulder, his eyes closed. Maybe she thought that this was the end, that they were done now that her son was safe. They were far from it, but he wouldn't tell her that. Not when she looked so relieved to be leaving the Lost Woods.

He stepped away from the four-wheeler, watching as Laurel drove away. He should be feeling relief, elation. The normal high that came from a successful mission. Instead, he felt worried, anxiety gnawing at him as he turned to the evidence team that was working the scene.

"Funny seeing her here," a short, wiry police officer said, his gaze on the retreating vehicle.

"Who?"

"Eva Billows. Last time I saw her, we were working her parents' murders. Shame that she's had so much trouble. Her father might have been a weasel, but she seems like a good kid.

"She mentioned her parents' murders."

"A bad scene. The bodies had been there for a couple of days before she found them."

The words sparked a memory—the murder of a couple in their double-wide trailer. The husband had been beaten and then shot execution-style. The wife had been shot in the chest. Their daughter had discovered the bodies when her mother hadn't shown up to babysit. The story had made local news because of the brutal nature of the crime and the horror of the young woman walking in on the scene. Austin hadn't worked the case, but he remembered the police station buzzing during the investigation.

"What were her folks' names?" He couldn't remember, but he thought there'd been some connection to a small-time drug ring. Some reason to believe that the crime had been retribution.

"Ernie and Tonya Billows," the officer said.

No wonder Eva's name had sounded familiar.

"Any leads on the case?"

"A few fingerprints that we couldn't match to anyone who didn't have an alibi. One or two sets that weren't in the system. No murder weapon. No suspects. The trail has gone cold, but that doesn't mean we're not still actively working it. Why?"

"I think what happened to Eva's son is connected to the attack on Captain McNeal's father and the theft of Rio, but if there are other avenues I need to check out, it would be good to know now."

"I don't think there is. Ernie was a small-time criminal. Not someone who would be remembered this long."

"What about his wife?" Austin queried.

"Just one of those sad women who got caught up with the wrong guy and couldn't ever quite disentangle herself from him. The way I see things, if you want to figure out who kidnapped the Billows boy, you just need to find out who this guy was working with." He gestured to the body.

"Hopefully, someone will track him down before he gets out of these woods and disappears into Sagebrush."

"You got a good look at him, right?" the officer asked.

"Not as good as I would have liked. Just what I called in over the radio. Dark hair. Medium build. Five-ten, max. Maybe a hundred and seventy pounds. No distinguishing features that I could see."

"I'll run that through the computer back at the station. We might get lucky and pull up someone you recognize. Internal affairs is going to want to interview you. From what I see, this was a clear case of self-defense and appropriate use of lethal force, but you know how these things work."

"All too well." Austin sighed.

"If you want to head back to the station, you can get the interview over with and get on with your day," the officer offered. "When I get back to the precinct, I'll email you the Billows file. You can look through it yourself. Maybe there's something we missed."

"Thanks." He called Justice, hooked the leash to his collar and scratched behind his ears.

Justice shook his big head, his ears flapping, his nose sniffing the air as if he were wondering what had happened to the prize he'd spent half the night searching for.

"You did good, boy," Austin said. "You found him. Now, all we have to do is keep him safe."

Justice cocked his head to the side, his dark brown eyes soulful. Then he barked as if he understood exactly what Austin was saying.

SIX

Twenty minutes of winding, bumpy pathways, a quick ride in an ambulance, an hour of doctors prodding and poking Brady while Eva answered an endless barrage of police questions, and finally...*finally*...it was over. Brady was settled under thick blankets, his blond hair brushed back from a bruised forehead, his eyes closed. Eva touched his scraped cheek, felt his still-cool skin. A few more hours, and he would have succumbed to hypothermia.

The thought made her physically ill.

She'd been so close to losing him.

Too close.

It felt like her fault. No matter how many times she told herself that it wasn't, she couldn't shake the feeling that she should have kept him safe.

In the years since her parents' murders, she'd done everything that she could to create a predictable routine and *normal* life for Brady. A life that was nothing like the one she'd had as a kid.

No police officers banging on the doors at all hours of the night. No hoodlums visiting in the wee hours of the morning threatening violence if a debt wasn't paid or a secret kept. All Eva wanted was to be a typical mother, doing typical things with her typical son. She didn't want drama. Didn't want danger. Didn't want any of the things that she'd grown up with.

A few more months of college and she'd have her teaching degree. She planned to apply to school districts far away from Sagebrush, Texas. Go somewhere north where there was snow and freezing weather in the winter. Where the days were longer in the summer and the air clear and crisp rather than humid. She planned to make a brand-new life where no one knew about her father.

But plans meant nothing if Brady wasn't part of them.

Her life.

Her heart.

Being his mother had forced her to become stronger. More self-sufficient. Much more patient and willing to wait on God's plans.

Most of the time.

Lately, she'd felt unsettled and discontent. As if the life she'd built for herself wasn't enough. As if there was something special waiting just around the corner. She'd wanted to run to whatever it was, grab it with both hands.

Instead, she just kept plodding along, doing the same things she'd been doing since Brady's birth—working as a waitress at Arianna's Café, going to school part-time, striving to provide a good life for her son.

She touched his cheek again, her chest tight. He still felt too cold. She pulled the covers up around his shoulders, wishing she could go home and get his favorite blanket. Wishing she could smooth the frown that marred his brow as he slept.

"Momma?" He opened his eyes. Looking in them was like looking into his father's. Only Rick's gaze had always been calculating, his smiles designed to disarm and manipulate.

"You okay?" She lifted Brady's hand, careful of the scrapes and cuts in his palm.

"I need to ask you something." His voice had a raspy quality that worried her. She wanted to ring for a nurse, demand that the doctor check on Brady again, but he was already hooked up to IV fluids, already warming up beneath a layer of blankets. There wasn't much more that could be done.

"What is it, sweetie?"

"Do you think they're going to come here?"

"Who?" she asked, but she knew, and the knowledge shivered through her.

"The bad men. Will they come to the hospital?"

"Of course not." She hoped. Prayed. Wanted to believe.

"How do you know?"

"There's a police officer sitting right outside the door. He'll keep the bad guys away."

"What if he doesn't?"

"He will, okay? The bad guys will be too scared to come around him."

"I wish Austin and Justice were there instead."

"They're busy."

"Looking for someone else who needs help?"

"Looking for the man who kidnapped you. They're going to put him in jail. Then you won't ever have to worry about him again."

"There were two men, Momma. Remember?"

She couldn't forget. The body lying beneath the blanket, the gun close beside it. Thank goodness Brady had been too tired to pay attention to the scene outside the cave. "They already took care of one of them."

"So, just one more?"

"Yes."

"Maybe Austin and Justice will come here after they find the bad guy."

"Sweetheart, they already helped us, and there are so many more people they can do that for."

"But they really liked me. Justice licked my hand and Austin even called me sport."

"Of course they liked you. *Everyone* likes you. But Austin and Justice have a very important job, and they don't have time to visit people at the hospital—"

Someone knocked, and Eva jumped, angling her body so she was between Brady and the door.

"Who is it?"

"Austin."

"I knew he would come! I knew it, Momma!" The hero worship in Brady's eyes was unmistakable, and Eva wanted to tell him not to put his hopes in Austin. He'd only be disappointed.

That was her life experience.

She didn't want to taint her son with it, but she didn't want him hurt, either.

"Come on in," she called, and Austin walked in.

No more police uniform. Just faded jeans and a fitted black T-shirt, his abs taut beneath the fabric. He had his leather bomber jacket under his arm and scuffed cowboy boots on his feet, and she didn't think she'd ever seen anyone look quite so good.

Her cheeks heated, and she looked away, refusing to acknowledge the butterflies in her stomach or the little skip of her heart when he moved close.

"How are you doing, sport?" he asked.

"My head hurts and my throat hurts and my knees hurt, too. They got all beat up when that mean guy pushed me and made me fall. See?"

Brady shoved all the blankets away and rolled up the little blue pajama pants that the hospital staff had dressed him in. Both of his knees were bandaged, one of them wrapped tight. A bruised kneecap, the doctor had said.

Eva hated to imagine the amount of force it would take to knock a child down so violently that his kneecap bruised.

"You need to stay warm, remember?" She slid the pant legs back down and pulled the covers back to his chin, her elbow bumping Austin's solid thigh.

She blushed again.

Called herself every kind of fool.

The man had saved her son. *Of course* she found him attractive. It didn't mean anything.

"I don't like all these blankets on me, Momma. I'm hot."

"Then why are your hands and cheeks cold?"

"Because…" He couldn't think of a good reason and fell back onto his pillow, his gaze jumping to Austin. "Where is Justice?"

"Home. He worked hard last night, and he needed a little time off."

"Momma said you were both out looking for the bad guy. She said you were going to throw him in jail so that he never came and got me again."

"Your mom is right. There are lots of police out looking for him."

"But you're here."

"I have to take a little vacation. Once I'm back at work, I'll be out looking for the bad guy every day."

"A vacation?" Eva asked even though she knew it didn't matter. As long as there were other officers working to protect Brady, she didn't need to know where Austin would be or what he'd be doing.

"Administrative leave." He dropped into a chair, not offering further explanation. It took a moment for the words to sink in.

"I'm sorry."

"It's nothing to do with you or Brady, Eva. It's just procedure. The way things are going, I should be back to work in a couple of days."

"That fast?" She wasn't sure she believed it, but then she'd made it a habit to *not* know how the police department worked.

"You've been interviewed by a police officer already, right?"

"Yes." She'd answered dozens of questions while the doctor examined Brady.

"He was from internal affairs. They're moving quickly on things because the investigation is fairly cut and dry, and because I'm lead investigator in another case."

"The one involving Slade's father?"

"That's right. There are other officers that can

take over if I can't proceed, but there's no reason to think I won't be able to. What happened was justified, and I followed protocol." He crossed his feet at the ankles. If being put on administrative leave bothered him, it didn't show.

She narrowed her eyes. "So, if you're on leave, why are you here?"

"To check on Brady."

"That wasn't necessary, Austin."

"Wasn't it?" he asked mildly, and she felt small and petty.

"I think it's my turn to apologize. I didn't mean that the way it sounded. After all that you've done, you're welcome to visit Brady anytime you want."

"And, next time, you're welcome to bring Justice," Brady said, and Austin chuckled, the sound as warm as a summer breeze and about ten times as nice.

"Not to the hospital, sport, but I'll bring him by your house once you get home."

"I don't know if Momma will let him come. She doesn't like dogs. She says they're mean and they bite."

"Not *all* dogs, Brady. I've told you that. Some dogs are perfectly nice." Eva's cheeks were pink, her gaze skittering away from Austin's.

He made her uncomfortable. He could see that, but he didn't plan on leaving. He might be on administrative leave, but that didn't mean he couldn't do a little investigating.

"But you said that we couldn't have a dog because we don't have the time for it and because they can be fishes and mean."

"Fishes?" Austin asked, and Eva offered a slight smile.

"*Vicious*. He's a typical seven-year-old. Sometimes he needs his ears cleaned out."

"And sometimes I need to plug them up." Brady yawned, his eyelids drooping, a dark bruise on his forehead livid against his pale skin.

"Why don't you close your eyes for a while?" Austin suggested, but Brady shook his head.

"I think you'll be gone when I wake up."

"Maybe I will be, but I'll come back again."

"You will?" Brady implored.

"Of course." He patted the little boy's hand, ignoring Eva's scowl. "And even better, if you sleep now, you'll get strong enough to go home a lot more quickly. Then I'll be able to visit you at your house."

"With Justice!" Brady made it sound like Austin had just offered the moon, and Austin's heart melted a little more than he wanted it to. A little more than he should allow it to.

He'd been down that road before.

It hadn't ended well.

He wouldn't go down it again.

"Yes," he responded, because he couldn't say no to Brady. He'd just have to be careful. Make sure that he didn't get pulled in any deeper than he already had been.

Brady nodded, but his eyes were already closed, his arm flung up over his head, an IV needle taped to it. A long scratch snaked from his wrist to his elbow and what looked like finger marks bruised the inside of his arm. His kidnappers hadn't been gentle with him. Of course, they probably hadn't expected that he'd be alive to complain to anyone.

"You don't have to come by to visit, Austin. I know that you were just trying to be kind, and I appreciate that, but I can tell Brady that you're busy. He'll understand," Eva whispered, and he looked into her eyes, felt the breath leave his lungs at the impact of that one glance.

He hadn't noticed how green her eyes were, how soft and misty. Hadn't noticed her flawless skin or her full, pink lips. He'd been working, and that had been his only focus. Now he was on leave, his focus on Brady and on Eva because it had nowhere else to be. Not his empty house. Not even his tired K-9 partner, who'd seemed more interested in lying on the sofa than playing a game of fetch in the backyard.

Truth be told, that's what had driven Austin to visit Brady.

He'd wanted to know that the seven-year-old

was okay, but he'd also wanted to reassure himself that what he did, the things that had kept him tied to his work and away from the life he'd always wanted to build, were worthwhile.

They were. He knew it, but there were times when he wanted more. A wife. Kids. A loud and busy house to go home to.

"If you want me to leave, Eva, I will." He stood, ready to walk out of the hospital, go back to his house and wait for the phone to ring and IA to give him the all-clear to go back to work. He needed to sleep anyway, catch up on the hours he'd missed while he was searching for Rio and for Brady.

"Wait." She touched his arm as he moved past, her fingers trailing heat as they slid away. "I..."

"What?"

"You don't have to leave. Brady has been dozing fitfully, and he could wake up any minute. If he does, he'll be happy if you're here."

"What about you?"

She shrugged. "I don't mind if you stay."

"You don't owe me anything, Eva. You don't have to allow me to be here out of some kind of obligation. If I make you uncomfortable—"

"You don't!" She protested a little too loudly, and Brady shifted in his sleep, turning on his side and moaning softly.

"You don't," Eva repeated in a hushed voice

as she brushed hair from Brady's forehead. She looked beautiful standing there, her expression as soft as her eyes, her lips curved into a small frown. Not as young as Austin had thought. Closer to thirty than to twenty.

"Knock, knock!" A female voice called, and the door opened. A tall, thin woman walked into the room, an oversize stuffed dog in her arms. Austin knew her. She owned Arianna's Café, a busy restaurant in the heart of downtown Sagebrush.

"Arianna! What are you doing here?" Eva's brow furrowed, her eyes shadowed and wary.

"You've been working for me since you were in high school. Did you think I wouldn't come visit your son while he was in the hospital?"

"How did you know he was here?"

"You're all over the news. I have to say, I'm a little upset that I didn't hear it straight from you, but I suppose you've been busy. How is he?" She approached the bed and dropped the dog onto the end of it.

"Hypothermic, bruised, still scared. Things could be worse, though."

"Of course they could. I hear that he was taken right out of his bedroom window. Not surprising that someone could break into your place like that. The house is nearly falling down, it's so old."

"It was built in the 1920s, Arianna, so it's not that old and it's not even close to falling down."

"It's not secure, though. You have to admit that. Maybe it would be best if the two of you came to my place for a while. I have a state-of-the-art security system, and with my work schedule, I'm not home that much. You'll have the place mostly to yourself."

"I appreciate the offer, but I'll get new windows and locks and have a security system installed at our place. We'll be fine."

"I hope you're right. If you change your mind, the offer will stay open. Perhaps this will help with the expense of having your house secured." She pulled an envelope from her purse and held it out. "I know that things are tight for you while you're in college."

"Arianna, I can't take that." Eva's gaze shot to Austin, her cheeks pink.

"Don't be silly. Of course you can. Besides, it's not just from me. When your coworkers heard that Brady was in the hospital, they took up a collection to help."

"Tell them that I really appreciate it." Eva took the envelope, but she didn't look happy about it.

"I'm sure that you'll be able to tell them yourself. You'll need a few days off, but I thought you could come in on Wednesday. That gives Brady five days to recover. I'm sure he'll be back in school by then."

"I—"

"You'll call me if there's a problem, but I'll assume that there won't be. I need to get back to the café." She hurried out of the room.

"Your boss, huh?" Austin watched as Eva tucked the envelope into her purse. She didn't open it. He wondered if she planned to use the money or to return it.

"Yes."

"You didn't seem thrilled to see her."

"I was just surprised." More than surprised. Eva had actually been shocked, but she didn't tell Austin that. She hadn't expected him, either. Hadn't really expected anyone but law enforcement and medical staff. She had friends at church, work and school, but she hadn't called any of them.

Do it yourself, hon. Whatever it is you want to accomplish, make sure you don't ever count on anyone else to help you achieve it.

She could hear her mother's words echoing from the past, and she walked to the bed, picked up the large, plush dog that Arianna had dropped there and placed it on one of the two chairs that sat near the window. It was just like Arianna to offer something so ostentatious. She enjoyed her status as benevolent benefactress when it suited her. Not that she wasn't a good boss; she was simply a demanding one.

"Nice dog." Austin touched the stuffed dog's head. "Food would be nicer. I don't know about you, but I'm starving. How about I get us both something from the cafeteria?"

"I'm not very hungry."

"Which means you *are* a little hungry." Austin smoothed his dark hair and offered a tired smile. He had circles under his eyes and the shadow of a beard on his jaw, and she could lose herself in his smile if she let herself.

"You go ahead and eat, but I'm fine."

"I'll be back in a few minutes." He left the room, left her just the way she'd thought she wanted to be—alone.

It didn't feel as good as she wanted it to.

She lifted the big white dog, hugged it to her chest, fighting back tears that she had no business shedding. Brady was safe. The police had promised to make sure he stayed that way.

They'd also promised to find her parents' killer.

She didn't want to think about that, or about what it might mean if they didn't follow through on their newest promise.

She wouldn't allow herself to imagine that Austin might somehow make things turn out differently than they had before. He seemed like a nice guy, a caring one. A person who could be depended on.

That didn't mean that *she* would depend on him.

Brady was her responsibility—his well-being,

his emotional health, all of it resting squarely on her shoulders. She couldn't risk his life or happiness on the hope that someone would help them. Just had to keep going on the way she had been, doing the best she could on her own.

SEVEN

Austin nodded to the police officer stationed outside Brady's door and walked down the hall. A bank of elevators stood across from the nurses' station, and he pressed the call button, waiting impatiently for the door to open.

He was hungry, tired and oddly anxious to return to Brady's room. It might have had something to do with Eva's misty green eyes and her soft smile.

"Austin!" Slade McNeal called out, and Austin pivoted, saw his boss hurrying down the hall toward him.

"I didn't realize you were here."

"It's where all the action is, so I guess it's the place to be," he said wryly.

"How is your father doing?"

"The same. Still in a coma but holding his own."

"I'm sorry, Slade. You know that I'm praying for him."

"I appreciate it." Slade smoothed his hair, which was just beginning to gray. The captain had been through a lot in the past few years, and it showed, but his passion for his job and his son hadn't changed. "Good job tracking Brady Billows. How is *he* doing?"

"He's exhausted and bruised, but there doesn't seem to be anything wrong with him that time won't heal."

"Glad to hear it. I got a call from internal affairs about a half hour ago."

"Yeah?"

"You should get cleared to return to work late tomorrow or the following day. In the meantime, Lee will work any leads we get on your cases. He'll keep you posted."

"Right now, Brady is the only lead we have. He witnessed the attack on your father and saw Rio being put into a van."

"My father said 'bay' before he lost consciousness. It's possible that he saw Brady and was trying to let us know that there was a witness."

"Knowing what we know now, I'd say it's more than possible. Was Lee able to find Jane Doe?"

"She was transported to the hospital about an hour ago. Lee tried to interview her, but she's barely lucid and says she doesn't know who she is or where she's from."

"You checked fingerprints and missing-persons reports?"

"Her fingerprints don't match anyone in the system. No one fitting her description has been reported missing. She may as well have fallen out of the sky."

"One more cog in the wheel, huh?"

"Unfortunately."

The elevator door opened and they stepped in.

"Are you heading home?" Austin asked.

"I have to. My son isn't doing well with Rio gone. He was up half the night crying, and the babysitter said that he's crying again. I don't feel right leaving him for too long."

"As soon as I'm given the clear, I'll get back on the case, Slade. You know that I'll do everything I can to find Rio quickly."

"That's why I asked you to take the lead."

"Who's taking the lead on the Billows case?" Austin queried.

"Since Brady has been found, I'm letting Cunningham handle closing the missing person's case. Eva has already been interviewed. We'll interview Brady when he's a little stronger."

"How about our deceased perp? Do we have an ID?"

"The medical examiner is going to pull prints, and we'll try to get a match. I'll let you know if we get a hit." They stepped off the elevator and walked to the exit. The sun shone bright beyond the glass doors, but clouds loomed large on the horizon. The rain would arrive soon, washing away scent trails and evidence.

Austin watched as Slade made his way across the parking lot, wishing he could have offered his friend more than words. He'd hoped to find Rio within an hour of getting the call that he'd been stolen, but they were eighteen hours out from the crime, and all he had was a dead perp, a description of another one and a seven-year-old witness.

More than he'd had the previous day, but not enough to make an arrest or to return Rio.

He grabbed a couple of sandwiches from the cafeteria, threw a couple of bags of chips on the tray with them. He grabbed a banana and an apple and tossed two packages of cookies in with the mix. Brady might like a snack later.

The cashier smiled a little too brightly as she rang him up, her bleached-blond hair brassy and her makeup just on the wrong side of subtle.

"You're a police officer, aren't you?" she asked as she slowly punched in the code for the banana.

"That's right."

"I knew it. Guy doesn't need to wear a uniform for me to recognize when he's in law enforcement. I'm intuitive that way."

"I'm sure you are," he muttered, and her smile broadened.

"Must be an exciting job, being a cop."

"It has its moments."

"Maybe we could get together sometime? You could tell me about it? I love everything that has to do with law enforcement." She beamed at him. "I'm always watching those true-crime shows at home. You know the ones I'm talking about?"

"Yes." He handed her cash and mentally hurried her through the process of counting out his change. A few years ago, her invitation would have flattered him, and he might have been tempted to take her up on it. He'd grown up a lot since his relationship with Candace had ended. Grown up and realized that a surface relationship with a pretty woman who liked his job more than she liked him was not what he wanted.

"So, what do you say? Want to get together after my shift? I get off at—"

"I'm sorry. Things are hectic right now, and my schedule is full."

"Oh." She handed him his change, looking more confused than upset. As if she couldn't quite figure out if she'd been rejected. "Maybe another time."

He didn't respond. Just thanked her and walked away.

Since he'd broken things off with Candace two years ago, he hadn't spent much time pursuing his old dreams. Family and forever tucked away in the old Victorian he'd spent the past five years restoring. He'd bought it planning to fill the rooms with kids and happiness, but work took him away more than any family deserved, and he'd given up the thought of having what he'd missed out on when he was a boy.

He knocked on Brady's door and pushed it open with his foot. The chair near the bed was empty, but Brady was exactly where he'd been when Austin had left, lying under thick blankets and sleeping deeply, his arm stretched above his head. He looked tiny and helpless, swallowed up by the bed and the room, and Austin felt the same softening of his heart that he'd felt earlier. He steeled himself against it the same way he had dozens of times before. Getting involved wasn't an option, but he couldn't seem to make himself put the food down and leave, either.

"You're back." Eva stepped out of the bathroom, her hair pulled into a high ponytail that showed off her slender neck and high cheekbones, her face dewy as if she'd just washed it.

Beautiful.

Very beautiful, and Austin's heart did more than soften, it burned hot in his chest.

"I told you that I would be." He dropped the food on the table, studied her pale face. The whole seemed greater than the sum of its parts. Large misty eyes, high cheekbones, a slightly-too-long nose speckled with freckles. Sharp chin, widow's peak and perfectly arched brows just a shade darker than her pale hair. She should have looked austere and unapproachable. Instead, she looked like the girl next door, everyone's best friend. The kind of person anyone would want on his side.

"People don't always do what they say. I'd think that someone in your line of work would know that." She shifted uncomfortably, fiddling with the end of her ponytail and avoiding his gaze.

"And *I'd* think that someone dealing with a person in my line of work would expect something different from him than what she'd expect from most people." He turned his attention to his sandwich, almost felt her relief, the sigh of her easing tension.

"Police are just like everyone else. We both know that." She smiled to take any sting out of the words. Nice, but guarded, that was the impression that Austin got, and he wondered what it would be like to push past the wall she'd built. See what lay on the other side of it.

"You're quite the cynic." He handed her a sandwich and settled into a chair beside the bed. He didn't have to work, so he might as well be there.

"Not really. I'm just a realist." She took the other chair, smoothed the covers on the bed, laid her palm against Brady's cheek.

"Because of what happened to your parents?"

"What about what happened to them?" She unwrapped her sandwich, a frown line marring the smooth skin of her forehead.

"Their murderer was never found. Maybe you blame the police for that. Think that we didn't work hard enough to find the killer. Maybe that's what's made you such a...realist when it comes to guys like me."

"I was a realist way before my parents' murders. Besides, you weren't part of the case at all, and the officers who were investigating did the best they could with what they had." She sighed. "Do I think they could have done more? Probably. But my father wasn't the kind of guy who endeared himself to law enforcement. I'm not sure they cared all that much about getting justice for him. I'm not sure I can blame them for that, either."

"What about getting justice for your mother?"

Her smile fell away, and she set the sandwich on the table. "What is it you want to know, Austin?"

"Nothing really." But he *was* curious about her family. About her criminal father and her mother. About the people who had made her the woman she'd become.

"Then why bring up my mother?"

"Someone mentioned her today. An officer who worked the case."

"What did he say?" She lifted the top piece of

bread off her sandwich and tossed a pickle into the trash can.

"That she was a nice lady who got caught up with the wrong man and could never quite free herself from him."

"That's one way to put it."

He raised a brow. "What's your way?"

"She fell in love with a man who was abusive and cruel, and she stayed with him until he killed her." Her words were cold, her eyes icy.

"You think your father killed your mother?" If so, it wasn't a theory he'd heard mentioned before.

"I think his crime got her killed, and I think that's pretty much the same thing." She took a bite of the sandwich, then wrapped it up again.

"Finished?"

"I've lost my appetite." An easy thing for Eva to do when she thought about her parents.

Two years, and she could still see her mother lying in a pool of blood, her eyes open and blank. Could still smell death, the scent of it filling the trailer where Eva had grown up. Still see the flies swarming in thick clouds above the bodies.

She gagged, nearly lost what little of the sandwich she'd eaten.

"Hey. It's okay." Austin pressed a cool palm to the back of her neck, urged her head down between her knees.

"I'm okay," she mumbled, but she wasn't sure

she was. It had been a long night, and she hadn't slept, and his cool palm felt like it was the only thing holding her to the world.

"Here. Drink this." He poured water from the pitcher and handed her the glass. She took a sip, flinching as he pressed a cold, damp towel to the back of her neck.

"That's cold."

"That's the point." He smiled, his eyes crinkling at the corners. Tired eyes and such dark blue that Eva thought they were exactly the color of the sky at midnight. They pulled her into their beauty just as easily, made her want to search for something more than the things she'd spent the past seven years striving for.

"Thanks." She nudged his hand away, holding the towel herself and crossing the room to stare out the window. She needed a little space to clear her head because he was starting to get to her. Starting to make her notice things that she hadn't noticed in a lot of years, that she hadn't ever planned to notice again.

Brady cried out, the sound breaking through Eva's thoughts, pulling her back to the room and her son.

"Brady?" She brushed soft hair from his forehead, smiling as his eyes opened. "How are you doing, buddy?"

"I had a bad dream."

"Did you?" Had he forgotten that it was all real? Did he think that everything that had happened was a nightmare? She almost hoped so. Would almost rather him believe that he'd had a nightmare than have him relive the terror.

"Yes. I dreamed the bad man came for me again. I dreamed he climbed right in the window and took me, and this time you didn't find me."

"I won't let that happen, Brady. I promise." She lifted his cold hand and smiled, but his attention was on Austin.

"I thought you left," he said.

Austin shook his head and stepped close to the bed. "Not yet."

"I'm glad. That bad guy won't come in the window while you're here."

"Even if I wasn't here, no one could get in the window. We're too high up."

"We are?"

"Sure. Want to see?"

"Okay." Brady pushed aside the covers, his little arms trembling, his movements uncoordinated. Bruises peeked out from under the cuffs of his pajama pants, the long scratch on his forearm angry and red.

"You need to stay in be—"

She didn't have a chance to finish. Austin lifted Brady from the bed and carried him to the window, rolling the IV pole beside him.

"See that? We're four stories up. The only way for the bad guy to get in this window would be for him to fly, and no one can do that."

"I guess you're right." Brady frowned, his head resting against Austin's shoulder, his eyes shadowed. He looked comfortable, his body relaxed, and Eva thought he might drift to sleep again. Right there in Austin's arms. Her palms itched to pull Brady away. Her mind screamed that she'd be making a big mistake if she didn't.

She wasn't the only one who could be hurt if she let Austin deeper into their lives. There'd been a time when she'd wanted nothing more than to know that her son would have a father and a mother raising him. She'd believed with everything in her that she and Rick were going to get married, that they'd have a beautiful house and a beautiful family.

That was before she'd learned that Rick was married.

Such a silly childish dream, and she'd outgrown it a long time ago. Still, seeing Austin and Brady together made her heart ache for all the things that might have been.

"You need to get back under the covers," she said, her voice husky and tight.

"I'm not tired, Momma." But his eyes were closed again.

Austin eased him back into bed and tucked the

covers up around his shoulders, the gentleness in his face adding to the ache in Eva's heart.

"You should probably go," she said, and he looked into her face, his expression unreadable.

She thought for a minute that he would find an excuse to stay, but he just nodded, dropped his business card on the table near the pile of food he'd brought. "If you need anything, call."

He walked out the door, closing it softly behind him.

Alone again. Eva and Brady. Just the way it was supposed to be. So why didn't she feel happier about it?

"Did he go, Momma?" Brady whispered.

"Yes," Eva murmured.

"I don't feel safe when he's not here." A tear slipped down his cheek, and Eva wiped it away, tried to tell herself that he'd be just fine. That she could be enough for him. That they didn't need anyone or anything but God and each other.

Somehow, though, that didn't seem quite as true as it had been the previous day.

EIGHT

Jeb Rinehart.

Austin stared at the name, tried to match it to the body that had lain in the stagnant pool near the cave. Twenty-seven. Red hair. Brown eyes. Sallow complexion. Three convictions on drug charges. Time served for the third one. Released from prison a month ago.

Dead by Austin's hand.

His cell phone rang, and he answered as he studied Rinehart's mug shot. "Black here."

"Austin? It's Eva."

"Is Brady okay?" He set the photo on his desk, glanced at his watch. An hour since he'd left the hospital, and he hadn't expected Eva to call at all, much less call so soon. There had to be a problem. A big one.

"He's fine." She sounded distracted.

"Do you need me to come back to the hospital?"

"No," she said too quickly.

"You do need something, though, right?"

"Not really. It's just that Brady has been talking about the kidnapping. I thought that I should let you know what he's been saying." Her words were hushed as if she didn't want her son to hear.

"What's that?" He grabbed a pad of paper and a pen, adrenaline pouring through him. He might be on administrative leave, but that didn't mean he couldn't jot down a few notes and pass them along to Slade.

"There may be a third man."

"Brady said that?"

"Yes. The two men who kidnapped him were arguing. That's how he managed to get away from them. The guy with the red hair wanted to shoot Brady and bury his body in the woods." Her voice broke, and Austin's grip tightened on the phone. It was all he could do not to get in his SUV and drive back to the hospital.

He wouldn't. He'd left because he'd known he couldn't stay and not start caring too much for Brady and Eva. He needed to stay away for the same reason.

An image of little Anna Lynn flashed through his mind, her dark eyes and curly dark hair. Her chubby cheeks and excited laughter. She'd called him Uncle Austin, and he'd carried her picture in his wallet, flashed it around like a proud relative. In his heart, that's what he'd been. He'd been best friends with Anna's father since elementary school, and he'd known Anna from the day she was born.

When he'd found her on the banks of a stream deep in the Lost Woods, a piece of his heart had torn apart.

"What else did Brady say?" he asked, his tone sharper than he'd intended.

"The dark-haired man said that he didn't want any part of killing a child. He'd been paid to take the dog, not commit murder. The red-haired man told him that they didn't have a choice. If they didn't kill Brady, The Boss would kill them instead."

"The Boss?"

"That's what Brady said."

"Anything else?" he probed.

"Just that the guy with the red hair got to yelling so loud that he forgot to hold on to Brady's wrist. Brady took off. It was still dark, so he was able to hide pretty easily. He found the cave a while later and hid in it until you and Justice found him."

"Brady is a smart kid."

She exhaled softly. "I know. I just wish…"

"What?"

"That none of this had happened. I wish we were at home enjoying a quiet day together. I wish that I didn't have to worry that someone was going to come after my son again."

"It's going to be okay," he said gently.

"You can't know that, Austin."

"You're right, but I'll do everything I can to make sure it's true."

"You're not even working the case right now." She cleared her throat. "I probably should have called someone else. I don't know why I didn't."

He thought she *did* know.

He knew.

Austin didn't believe in soul mates, but when he'd looked into Eva's eyes at the hospital, he'd felt a moment of recognition so intense that he'd thought that they must have met years ago, been friends for a long time rather than simply acquaintances for a few hours. Something had jumped to life in the depth of her gaze. He'd seen it. Had known that she'd told him to leave because of it.

Attraction, chemistry, he could stick any name to it that he wanted, and it would still be there. That didn't mean he had to act on it.

"We spent hours searching for your son together. That's plenty of reason for you to call me, Eva."

"I just...don't want to put you out." She sighed, and Austin imagined her fiddling with the end of her ponytail and staring out the hospital window.

"You're not, *and* you did the right thing in calling me. I'll pass the information on to Slade. He may want to stop by tomorrow to question Brady."

"He'll have to stop by our place. The doctor came in a few minutes ago. He thinks that Brady will be well enough to go home tomorrow morning."

"That must be a relief," Austin said.

"It is. I think we'll both feel better when we're back at home."

"Just make sure you get the security company out to your place quickly."

"I have an appointment set up for tomorrow afternoon," she confirmed. "The company can install the windows, locks and the security system. Hopefully, that will be enough to keep Brady safe."

"It's a good start. You might also want to consider getting a dog."

"Did Brady pay you to say that?"

"No, but I'm sure that he would have tried if he'd thought of it."

"For someone who just met him, you know my son well." She laughed softly, the sound as warm as a sun-drenched spring day.

"He's not shy about his desire to get a puppy, so I guess I can't take credit for a better-than-average ability to read people."

"Actually, I think you probably have a way better-than-average ability to do that. I'd better let you go. I'm sure you have a busy day planned." No more humor in her voice. No more laughter.

She disconnected, and he was left with the phone pressed to his ear, the pad of paper still sitting on the desk. He jotted a couple more notes, typed a quick email to Slade. He'd call him, too, but the information would be in the computer, and easy to access once the captain got his son settled down.

Austin glanced at his notes and frowned, circling the words that interested him most.

Paid to take the dog.

The Boss.

Kill them instead.

If Brady had heard right, someone who'd had money and power had been calling the shots yesterday.

"I thought you were on leave, Austin. Shouldn't you be home catching up on some sleep?" Valerie Salgado said.

The newest member of the Sagebrush Special Operations K-9 Unit, she came from a long line of police officers and seemed more than capable of following in the footsteps of her family. There was a softness about the rookie cop that surprised Austin, though. An openness that he hoped wouldn't be changed as months on the police force turned into years.

"I was heading that way. I just stopped in to see if the medical examiner had ID'd the deceased perp."

"Did he?" Valerie asked.

"Yes. The guy's name was Jeb Rinehart. He's served time. Was just released a few weeks ago."

"Probably would have been better for him if he'd stayed in jail." Valerie tucked a strand of long red hair behind her ear and lifted the mug shot, then leaned over Austin's shoulder and read the notes he'd written.

"Who's that?" She jabbed at *The Boss*.

"Brady Billows says that The Boss was calling the shots on Rio's theft and on Brady's kidnapping." He filled Valerie in on the information that Brady had given Eva, and she frowned.

"The victim is seven?"

"Right."

"It's easy for a kid that age to confuse information that he hears. Especially when he's under stress."

"True." But the story Brady had told was detailed, and Austin couldn't imagine that it was a product of confusion.

"But you don't think he's confused?"

"No," he said.

"If he's not, then we've got a big problem. The only way to solve it is to find the second kidnapper." She glanced at him. "What was Rinehart in jail for? Maybe we can search the database for guys who match the description you gave this morning and who have similar rap sheets to his."

"Drugs. Selling and possession."

"In that case, we might want to check with Parker."

"Check with me about what?" Parker Adams called from his desk.

"You've got some good ears, you know that, Parker?" Valerie responded.

"Only when my name is being mentioned. Who's the perp?" Parker joined them in Austin's cubicle, his dark hair slightly mussed. An undercover narcotics detective with the K-9 Unit, he knew most of the drug dealers in Sagebrush and had an ear to the pulse of the drug underground.

"Jeb Rinehart."

"I know the name. We put him away two years ago. The guy is—"

"Was," Austin cut in, and Parker frowned.

"He's your dead perp?"

"Yes."

"I'm surprised that he was involved in something that he was willing to take a bullet for. He was a small-time thug who was more interested in where he was going to get his next fix than in anything else."

"According to his kidnapping victim, Rinehart was afraid for his life," Austin explained, offering the information that Brady had provided.

"We need to find the guy he was working with. Pauly Keevers may be able to help us on that. Want me to put the word out on the street that you're looking for information?" Parker asked.

"If you think that he has information about Rinehart's friends, then, yes."

"Is there a criminal in Sagebrush who Pauly doesn't have information about?" Valerie asked. A good question. A street thug who liked to play both sides of the fence, Keevers was in the business of exchanging information for money.

"Probably not, but Keevers and Rinehart live in the same apartment complex. If I know Keevers, he knows everything there is to know about the people who live in his building. Friends. Family. Secrets. He'll know who Rinehart hung with, and he'll know who he might have been working for. For a price, he'll share that information." Parker sounded excited, and Austin had to admit, his adrenaline was pumping, too. They finally had a name, a face, a little bit of information that might lead them to more information.

"Sounds like a plan, Parker."

"Now that I'm thinking about it," Parker continued. "There's another guy you might want to talk to. Name is Camden West. He was arrested the same time as Rinehart. Booked on possession, distribution and possession of an illegal firearm. He's doing nine years in the state prison.

He and Rinehart were high school buddies. Next-door neighbors."

"Cell mates?" Valerie asked.

"Doubtful, but if anyone knows what Rinehart was involved in, it's Camden West."

"I'll pay him a visit," Austin cut in.

"You're forgetting that you've been put on leave, Austin," Valerie reminded him.

"Not forgetting. Just choosing to believe that I'll be off it soon."

"If not, I'll make the visit for you. Speaking of which, I've got to do a follow-up interview with Susan Daphne."

"Brady's babysitter?" Austin wanted to be the one to interview her. Wanted to be deep into the investigation rather than heading home to catch up on sleep.

"Slade thought Brady might have mentioned something to her or that she might have heard something around the time she sent him out to walk her dog. He asked me to handle interviewing witnesses until you're reinstated."

"Thanks," Austin said, but he wasn't happy about letting Valerie or anyone else handle any part of the case he'd been assigned. He didn't start something and stop. He kept going until he found what he was looking for.

Rio. Brady's kidnapper. The Boss. *Answers.* Lots of answers.

He turned off his computer, grabbed his coat from the back of his chair and walked outside.

Thick clouds covered the sun, their steel-gray color matching Austin's mood. He needed to get home, catch a few hours of sleep. Tomorrow was a new day, and it would bring its own set of problems.

The thought of going home didn't thrill him—the empty Victorian about as appealing as a steam bath on a summer day. Justice was there, of course, but talking to a dog wasn't the same as talking to a person. Someone who asked questions, exchanged ideas, wanted more than a game of fetch, a bowl of dog chow and a belly rub.

He hopped into his SUV, tempted to drive to the hospital and check on Brady one last time. Only Brady was fine. He had an armed guard stationed outside his door, a mother who would give her life for him, a K-9 unit searching for his kidnapper. As long as he stayed in the hospital, the potential for danger was minimal.

So maybe Eva was really the person Austin wanted to see.

Her soft green eyes and softer smile. Her quiet laughter and guarded heart. Vulnerable but tough. That appealed to him more than he wanted it to. *She* appealed to him.

He'd admit it, but he wouldn't act on it.

Not now.

Probably not ever.

Because his life was about his work, his focus on his job. He couldn't be any other way, and that wasn't something that the women he'd dated had ever been able to understand.

Candace had been the last woman that he'd tried for. After her, he'd decided that casual dating was easier than long-term commitment and planning for the future.

But it was also emptier. Lonelier.

He frowned, turning up the radio and trying to drown out the thought.

He had a good life. A great one. He'd been blessed to have a mother who'd raised him by herself, but who'd known the meaning of sacrificial love. He'd learned a lot from her example, and he'd been determined to pull himself out of the poverty that he'd been born into, to make something of himself, to contribute to the community and to the world. It had taken time, hard work and dedication, but he'd done it. If his mother had lived, she would have been proud.

She'd also have told him that there was more to life than work. More to happiness than a job or financial success.

She'd have been right, but Austin's course was set, and he didn't plan to veer from it.

No matter how tempting Eva might be.

NINE

Maybe another night in the hospital would have been best, Eva thought as she chopped onions for soup stock. Brady sat silent and morose at the kitchen table, his skin so pale it was almost translucent.

"You need to eat some of your sandwich, sweetie," she said, tossing the onions into the pot.

"I'm not hungry, Momma."

"I know that you don't *feel* hungry, but the doctor said you need to eat. If you don't, you might end up back in the hospital."

He sighed and took a tiny bite of sandwich, the bruise on his forehead deep purple. The scratches on his cheek looked raw, and his battered knees peeked out from beneath faded pajama shorts. He hadn't wanted bandages, and she'd let him have his way. They were both grumpy from too little sleep, and choosing her battles had seemed like the right thing to do.

She tossed diced carrots in with the onions,

threw celery in on top of that. A big pot of chicken noodle soup would last most of the week. A good thing since money would be tight for a while. The security system and new locks had cost a small fortune, and despite her coworkers' donation, Eva hadn't been able to afford new windows. She'd have to pinch pennies in order to have them installed, and that's exactly what she planned to do.

She also needed to write a thank-you note to her coworkers and bake some cookies to bring in for the café's staff on Wednesday. But all she really wanted to do was get through the day, tuck Brady into bed, lie down beside him and sleep until the sun came up.

She glanced at the clock.

Three in the afternoon.

They had a long way to go before either of them would be going to bed.

"I think that I'm finished, Momma. May I go play with my blocks?" Brady slid his plate away, the sandwich barely touched. She'd made his favorite, too. Grilled cheese with ham.

"As soon as I finish this." She placed a large stewing chicken into the pot and poured water over it.

"I can play in the living room by myself, Momma." Brady scowled.

He was right.

Logically, she knew it.

But she hadn't been logical since she'd walked into his bedroom and seen his empty bed and open window.

"I know you can, but how about you give me a hand, instead? Find the big lid that we use for the stew pot, okay?"

He moved like an old man, crossing the small kitchen and bending gingerly to look through the cupboard next to the stove.

"Never mind, buddy. I'll find it." She crouched beside him, touching his forehead, his cheek, his scratched-up hand. "You go ahead and play with your blocks. Just make sure that you stay in the living room. No going outside or anything."

"I won't. I promise." He offered a tiny smile, nothing like the full-out ones he usually gave, and limped from the room.

She had to force herself not to follow.

He'd be okay in the living room, the curtains pulled closed over the windows, the door locked, a police cruiser parked at the curb in front of the house.

Slade had promised twenty-four-hour protection until Brady's kidnapper was caught, and so far, he'd followed through. He'd had two patrol cars escort her home, a police officer walk her inside and search the entire house.

Eva shouldn't feel as if Brady could disappear at any moment, but she did.

She peered into the living room, watching as Brady dumped a small plastic container full of blocks onto the floor. He looked so little, so vulnerable.

An image flashed through her mind. Brady at the hospital, cradled in Austin's arms. He'd looked safe there. Protected.

She shoved the image away, stalking back to the soup pot, adding salt and pepper and digging the lid out of the cupboard. She turned down the gas, left the stock to simmer. A few hours and she could remove the chicken. If Brady was up to it, he could help her peel chicken from the bones.

The doorbell rang, and she jumped.

"Don't answer it, Brady!" she yelled as she wiped her hands on a dishcloth and ran into the living room.

Brady sat wide-eyed on the floor, his eyes shadowed, his body still. She'd never wanted to see terror on her son's face, but she saw it now, and she wanted so much to turn the clock back, be in his room when the kidnappers tried to take him, protect him so that he never had to know the kind of fear she'd lived with as a child.

"Who is it, Momma?"

"I don't know." She looked out the peephole, saw dark hair and midnight-blue eyes.

Austin.

Her heart leaped for him, but she refused to admit just how pleased she was to see him.

"Hold on!" She turned off the alarm, opened the door and let him in.

She'd spent most of the night telling herself that Austin wasn't anything like she remembered him to be. Not as handsome. Not as strong. Not as compelling.

She'd been wrong.

He was even more of all of those things.

Justice padded along beside him, his nose to the wood floor, his long ears brushing through the dust that she hadn't had a chance to sweep up. He lumbered across the room, sniffing Brady's hair and his neck.

Brady giggled, patting the fur near Justice's neck.

"I think my son has found a new best friend," Eva said, closing the door and dropping onto the sofa, more relaxed than she'd been in hours. She didn't bother thinking about what that meant, just enjoyed the feeling of not being alone and not being scared.

"I think Justice has found a new best friend, too," Austin responded with a smile as Justice plopped his head onto Brady's legs and looked at him adoringly. "Want me to call him off?"

"And devastate them both? I don't think so."

"Good, because I'm beat, and I'd rather just

sit here and watch them smile at each other." He dropped onto the sofa beside her despite the fact that the old rocking chair would have been a perfectly good seat.

Eva could have moved.

She didn't.

Just sat there feeling his warmth despite the fact that they weren't touching, inhaling winter air and spicy cologne. He smelled like the outdoors, only better, and that was something she should definitely not be noticing.

"It sounds like Brady and I weren't the only ones who didn't sleep well last night."

"I slept well. Then I decided that since I had some time off, I'd do some work on my house. I spent the morning refinishing the hardwood floor on the first level. The old muscles aren't used to all that work." He stretched his arms above his head and winced, his biceps bulging against soft cotton.

His muscles were anything but old.

Her cheeks heated, and she turned her attention back to Brady and Justice. "Do you really think Justice is smiling, because he looks more like he's frowning to me?"

"Don't let his hangdog expression fool you, Eva. Justice is almost always smiling. Aren't you, boy?"

Justice didn't raise his head, but his tail thumped.

"I suppose that he's so well trained that he helped you finish your floors. Maybe even handled a room all by himself."

"I wish. He spent most of the time lying in a sunny spot on the back porch." Austin laughed, the sound rumbling through the sofa cushions and settling somewhere in the vicinity of Eva's heart.

"Do you have any idea when the two of you will be back on the job?" she asked, shifting a little, trying to put more distance between them. His scent followed her, his heat still seeming to seep into her bones, warm her as nothing had in a very long time.

"I got a call from internal affairs this morning. They've almost completed their investigation. As soon as they do, I'll be back at work."

"I'm glad. I hate to think that you're on leave because of me and Brady."

"Not because of either of you. Because of Jeb Rinehart."

"Who?"

"The red-haired thug who kidnapped Brady."

"You were able to identify him?"

"The medical examiner took his prints. We were able to match them through our data bank."

"How about his partner?" she asked.

"Nothing yet."

She bit her lip. "Too bad. I was hoping this would all be over quickly."

"It still could be. We're only twenty-four hours out."

"That's a lifetime when your child is in danger."

"I know," he said and sounded like he really did. "We're doing everything that we can to make sure Brady stays safe until we find the person responsible for his kidnapping."

"I'm just…worried. He's scared, and he's not sleeping. He woke from nightmares so many times last night, I lost track of the number." She sighed wearily. "It's not just the physical injuries that I'm worried about. It's the emotional stuff. No parent wants to see her child suffer."

"I know that, too." His gaze was on Brady, his eyes shadowed and dark, his lips pressed tight as if he knew exactly how it felt to care so deeply about someone that nothing else mattered.

"Do you have children, Austin?" she asked and regretted the question immediately. Too personal. Not her business. Something someone only asked when she cared a lot about the answer.

"I haven't had time for marriage or family. My job is pretty intense, and I spend a lot of time away from home. It just didn't seem fair to bring a wife and kids into that."

"People do it all the time." She really *did* need to stop talking.

"So maybe the real truth is that I just haven't met a woman I'd want to build a family with." He studied her face, his gaze a physical touch that lingered on her eyes, her cheeks, her chin, landed briefly on her lips and then slowly moved away.

"I'd better check on my stock." She jumped up, her cheeks fiery, but he snagged her hand, pulled her back down.

"There's no need to run, Eva."

"I'm not," she muttered, but she settled back into her seat, her long legs folded under her, a knee poking out from a hole in her jeans. She'd braided her hair, and it fell in a long rope over her shoulder. Neat as a pin, and Austin had the absurd desire to loosen it up.

"Could have fooled me." He stood, stretching the kinks from his muscles and putting a little distance between them. He hadn't stopped by to make a play for Eva. The opposite was true. He'd stopped by to convince himself that what he'd felt when he'd looked into her eyes was nothing more than imagination brought on by exhaustion.

He'd been wrong.

"I wasn't running, and I do need to check on my soup stock, but I guess you didn't just stop by to see how Brady was doing. So why don't you tell me why you *are* here." She pulled her knees to her chest, wrapped her arms around her shins. Her knuckles were red and a little raw, the skin cracked. She worked hard and it showed, and that appealed to Austin way more than he thought it should.

"Your parents' case file was emailed to me this morning. I spent a little time looking through it."

"And?" She seemed to sink into herself, her eyes suddenly distant, the misty green faded to a muted hazel.

"Jeb Rinehart was mentioned in it." That had been a surprise, and Austin hadn't been able to accept it as coincidental.

"I'm not surprised," she admitted.

"No?"

"I'm sure you've seen my father's record. He dabbled in just about anything that could make him money, and most of the things he dabbled in were illegal."

Austin *had* seen it. Ernie's rap sheet had been several pages long. Mostly petty stuff that couldn't keep him in jail for long. A few domestic-violence charges that had been dropped by his wife before they'd ever gone to trial. "Your father did seem to have an affinity for trouble."

"He also had an affinity for alcohol and temper tantrums."

"You weren't close?"

"We weren't even in the same universe." She sighed, rubbed the back of her neck. "Look, Ernie had one goal in life—to make himself happy. He did whatever he wanted, whenever he wanted, and he didn't care who he hurt in the process. The fact that he was somehow connected to a guy who'd be willing to kidnap and mu—" Her gaze cut to Brady. "It's not a surprise."

"Do you remember your father ever mentioning Rinehart?"

"No. Never. But I wasn't a part of his life after Brady was born."

"How about your mother?"

"We were close, but Ernie was always first with her. If she'd ever had to choose between him and me, I knew what her decision would be. I guess, in the end, that's what happened." She smiled, her eyes sad.

She'd grown up hard.

Just looking at her father's police record proved that.

"I'm sorry."

"For what?"

"Stirring up old memories."

"You're doing your job. You don't have to apologize for that." She stood and stretched, offering a tired smile. "I really had better go check on my soup stock before it boils over."

She walked from the room, and Austin was sure that she wished she could walk away from her past easily.

He heard her moving around, silverware clinking, water running. Domestic noises that seemed so much homier when someone else was making them.

He didn't follow.

She needed space. He'd give it to her, but he had more questions he wanted to ask. About the case. About her father.

About her.

"Do you want to play blocks with me?" Brady asked, and Austin dropped down onto the floor beside him, worried by his paleness and the somberness in his eyes. Kids shouldn't be scared, and he was. That wasn't okay. Not by a long shot.

"Sure. What are you building?"

"A jail. I'm going to put all the bad guys in it."

"Good thinking. You build the jail. I'll find the bad guys and lock them inside it."

"Will you throw away the jail key?"

"Isn't that the way it's always done?" He pressed a block into place and Brady grinned, some of his anxiety seeming to slip away.

"Yes!"

"Then let's get to work. Where do you want this one?" He handed Brady a long gray block, smiling as he snapped it into place.

Maybe he couldn't be on the case yet, but he *could* provide a little distraction for a kid who obviously needed it.

And right at that moment, that seemed just as important as anything else he could be doing.

TEN

Brady's laughter drifted into the kitchen, Austin's warm chuckle following right behind it.

Eva tried to ignore both.

She couldn't.

Somehow, in the short amount of time he'd been alone with Brady, Austin had managed to do something that Eva hadn't been able to do in an entire day—distract Brady from his fear.

She frowned, staring into the stew pot, the chicken bobbing in the golden liquid. Looking at it made her stomach churn. A migraine nudged at the back of her head. She rubbed the spot, pressing her fingers into taut tense muscles.

"Headache?" Austin's words startled her, his silent entrance into the kitchen a surprise.

She met his gaze, found herself lost in midnight skies and starry vistas. She'd never seen eyes like his. Ever.

"A little." She stood on her toes, grabbed a generic pain reliever from the cupboard above the fridge, her hands shaking for reasons she refused to acknowledge. She couldn't pop the lid, and Austin took it.

"Let me help." He flipped open the cap with enough ease to make her cheeks heat.

"Thanks. It was a long night, and I'm still exhausted."

"Maybe you should take a page from Brady's book and lie down for a while." He leaned his hip against the counter, his broad frame taking up more than its fair share of room in the tiny kitchen. She scooted past, filling a glass with water and chugging it down with the pain reliever.

"He's lying down?"

"Yes. We built a block jail, and then his eyelids started drooping. I figured it was time for him to get some sleep."

"I better check on him."

"Justice is with him. He'll alert if there's anything to worry about." He snagged her wrist, pulling her back when she would have walked out of the kitchen.

"Austin—"

"Relax, Eva. I just want to ask you a few more questions." His hand dropped away. She was free to leave the kitchen or to stay.

Or maybe not.

Because her feet felt glued to the floor, her gaze

stuck to his, and no matter how many times her brain said that she should go, her heart said that she should stay. "What questions?"

"Brady mentioned a third party that Rinehart and his partner were working for. I'm wondering if your father could have been working for him, too."

"Ernie always worked for someone. He lacked the drive and initiative to ever make a go of things on his own."

"Do you remember him mentioning a particular job or name?"

"We weren't on speaking terms when he died," she said flatly.

"How about your mother? Did she—"

"My mother had nothing to do with my father's crimes." Eva had said that a hundred times after the murders. Ernie might have deserved what he'd gotten, but Tonya had been an innocent bystander, killed simply because of who she had been married to.

"I know she didn't. Everyone on the force knows the same. Your mother was in the wrong place at the wrong time, and she died because of it. It's a horrible thing, Eva. Everyone agrees, but it's possible that she did know the person who killed her, and it's possible she knew why," Austin replied, the gentleness in his voice making her eyes burn and her throat ache.

No way would she cry.

Not in front of him.

Crying is for babies, kid, and you're not that. Keep those tears flowing, and I'll give you something to cry about. Ernie's voice seemed to taunt her from the past, the words ones she'd been hearing for nearly three decades.

"Mom has been dead for over two years. Whatever she knew is gone with her. Whoever she saw in those last moments, it was my father she reached for. When I found their bodies, she was holding his hand. She'd been shot in the chest, and instead of grabbing the phone and calling for help, she reached for him, held on to him." She shoved the memory away, dropping into a chair, suddenly so tired, she didn't think her legs would hold her.

"I'm sorry. Again."

"You don't need to be. You just need to know that my mother was more loyal to my father than to anything else. Even if she'd known who he was working for, she'd never have told anyone."

"All right." He straightened, staring into her eyes. She thought that he planned to sit in the chair next to hers, ask questions that had nothing to do with her parents or the case. Maybe tell her about his life, his day, his job.

She wanted that.

Wanted it so much that she knew she had to send him away.

"I'm beat. I probably should lie down for a while." She forced herself to stand.

"Then I'd better get out of your hair." Austin didn't want to, though. He wanted to stay a while longer. Sit in the warm kitchen, inhaling the savory aroma of the stock that simmered on the stove and talking to Eva.

He walked into the living room, grabbed his coat from the couch and slipped it on. He'd spent the past seven years working on the police force and volunteering as a search-and-rescue worker. He was used to being busy. Used to working cases, being around coworkers, spending weekends training.

He wasn't used to idle time. Having it obviously didn't suit him. He dreaded taking Justice back to their quiet house. Dreaded another evening spent in front of the TV. Dreaded facing the part of himself that still longed for something to fill the downtime. Some*one* to fill it.

"Are you leaving already, Austin?" Brady asked sleepily, his small frame splayed out on the couch. Justice was scrunched in next to him, his big tan head on Brady's legs. They looked so comfortable and content, Austin hated to separate them.

"I'm afraid so."

"Does Justice have to go with you?"

Austin nodded. "Yes. He needs to eat dinner and spend some time running around in our backyard."

"Are you going to run around with him?"

"I'll probably throw the ball for him a couple of times. He loves to play fetch."

"I could throw the ball for him. I love to play fetch, too!"

Austin chuckled. "Sorry, buddy, but I don't think you're up to that. Maybe another day."

"Okay. So after you and Justice play fetch, are you going to look for the bad guy?"

"Not yet. I'm still on vacation, but I have some buddies who are working really hard to find the guy who kidnapped you."

"You're the best, though." Brady's eyes were wide and blue and so filled with sincerity that Austin had to smile.

"So are you."

"Can you visit me again tomorrow?"

"He's really busy, Brady," Eva responded before Austin could.

"Not so busy that I can't stop in and see a friend. Unless you'd rather I not?" He looked into Eva's eyes, saw his own confusion in the depth of her gaze. Almost wished that she'd tell him to stay away. Mostly wished that she wouldn't.

Don't get emotionally involved. Don't give yourself a chance to lose another piece of your heart.

That's what he'd been telling himself for twenty-four hours.

The problem was, he wasn't listening.

"Austin..." Eva began.

"What?"

She glanced at her son. "Nothing. I guess we'll see you tomorrow."

"See you then," he responded as he opened the front door, walked out into cold winter air. It cooled the heat that flowed through him every time he was with Eva, reminded him of his humanity.

He could fail Brady and Eva so easily.

He could do everything in his power to make sure that Brady stayed safe, to track down his kidnapper, to give him back the life he'd had before Rio was stolen. He could work endless hours and devote every waking moment to it and things could still turn out badly.

He acknowledged that, but he also acknowledged that he had no choice but to follow through. To give as much as he had to keep Brady safe. It was what he did, and he couldn't turn his back on it any more than the sun could decide not to rise in the morning.

He let Justice into the back of the SUV, then climbed into the driver's seat, turning up the vol-

ume of the radio as he backed out of the driveway. Eva's living-room curtains fluttered and
then moved aside. Austin thought Brady would be
standing there, thought that he'd have to call Eva
and tell her to keep her son from the windows.
She stood there instead, her long braid hanging
over her shoulder in a silky rope of gold.

She lifted a hand, and he returned the wave. Felt
his heart catch and his mind go because he wanted
to see the same thing when he left his own place
every morning. Wanted to head out to work knowing that someone was waiting for him to return.

Not a good direction for his mind to be heading.

He was happy with his life.

Happy with his work.

Happy, but he thought that maybe he could be
happier.

A family, children, love.

Those were things that everyone craved.

He sighed, ran a hand down his jaw.

In the past few years, all Austin had done was
run from one case to the next, one missing person
to the next. He'd tracked and trailed and hunted,
and he didn't have one regret.

He wanted more, though.

So much more than a job and a house and
friends.

Unfortunately, right at that moment, those were
his only options. Most of his friends were busy

with their families and Saturday plans. His house still stunk from the layers of varnish he'd applied to the floor, and his coworkers would probably boot him out the door if he showed up at the office again.

That didn't mean he couldn't keep busy and help with the case. As a matter of fact, he could pay a visit to Jeb Rinehart's buddy Camden West and start things moving in the direction he planned to take them once internal affairs allowed him to return to work.

He drove a few houses up the road, parked behind Slade McNeal's SUV and got out.

"Want to visit an old friend?" he asked Justice as he opened the back of the SUV and let him out. Justice raised his head, took a long deep sniff of air and barked enthusiastically. He knew where they were. They'd been there dozens of times before.

This time, though, Rio wouldn't be around to play with.

His father, Chief, would be, though. A retired service dog, he'd been one of the best. Now he was a family pet, enjoying his golden years.

He probably missed Rio. Slade's son, Caleb, was missing him, too. At five years old, Slade's little boy had already lost his mother in a bombing that had been meant for Slade. Two years later, he was still struggling to come to terms with that loss. Losing Rio had to have set him back in his recovery.

Maybe a visit with Justice would cheer Caleb up, and while they were visiting, Austin would try to talk Slade into letting him pay a visit to the state prison. Camden West had some information that Austin was interested in, and the sooner he got it, the happier he'd be.

Sure, he wasn't officially on duty, but that didn't mean he couldn't pursue a lead.

He rang the doorbell and waited for Slade to open the door.

ELEVEN

Two hours later, he was on his way, darkness sliding across the horizon as he made the ninety-mile trek to the state prison, his uniform crisp and comfortable, his firearm in its holster.

Back at work.

Slade had been excited to give him the news, and Austin had been happy to hear it.

Internal affairs had deemed the case cut-and-dried. Austin had acted appropriately and according to the guidelines set up by the office. A witness had confirmed it. Bullets from the deceased's gun had been found in and around the cave where Eva and Brady had been hiding. Because the perp had refused to lay down his firearm, Austin had been given no choice but to use deadly force.

He'd known that he'd acted according to policy, but it felt good to know that others agreed.

It felt even better to be on the job again, searching for Brady's kidnapper and for Rio.

Slade's house had felt emptier without the German shepherd in it, and the weight of Austin's responsibility to his friend, his boss, his team weighed heavily on his shoulders. Forty-eight hours without a good lead, and the case was going cold fast.

Maybe his visit with Camden West would be the key to heating it back up again. If West and Rinehart had been as close as Parker seemed to think, there had to be some interesting information to glean from it. One name. That's all Austin needed. If he got it, he could run with it and hopefully run straight into The Boss.

His cell phone rang as he pulled up to the prison gates and handed the guard his ID. He ignored it as he was waved into the parking area.

Moments later, it rang again.

He answered quickly, anxious to get into the building and start his meeting. "Austin Black."

"I hear you're looking for some information." The voice was vaguely familiar. Austin's pulse jumped, adrenaline pulsing through him. The fish had finally taken the bait. All he had to do was reel in the line.

"Pauly Keevers, right?"

"You guessed it, Detective. So, *are* you looking for information or not?" A small-time criminal with his fingers in more pies than Austin cared to count, Pauly would do just about anything for a buck, including selling out friends and family.

Bad news for Pauly's associates, but good news for the Sagebrush Police Department.

"That depends on what information you have to offer. Do you know Jeb Rinehart?"

"Knew him. I heard you blew out his brains, though, so I guess we'd better keep things past tense. Me? I'm in no mood to meet up with him in the afterlife, so I think I'll try to stay on your good side, Detective."

"Were you and Rinehart close friends or not?"

"I wouldn't say we were friends. We lived in the same apartment building."

"Did you talk to him much?"

"Nah. He kept to himself. Had a temper, the way I hear it. That's not the kind of person I want to associate with. Too dangerous."

And betraying friends for money wasn't?

Austin kept the thought to himself, leaning back in his seat and staring out at the purple-black night.

"I'm sure that didn't keep you from collecting information about the guy."

"I'm in the business of information, Detective. You know that."

"So you know who Rinehart hung out with?" Austin pressed.

"I do."

"Do you also know that Rinehart kidnapped

a young boy? That he's a suspect in an attack against Captain McNeal's father, and that—"

"He's suspected of stealing the captain's police dog? Yeah, I know. I know lots of things."

"Like?"

"Come on, Detective, you know me better than that." Keevers's mocking laughter drifted across the line.

"How much is it going to take to get you to talk?"

"That depends on what you want me to talk about."

Austin clenched his jaw. "I told you that I'm not in the mood for games, Pauly."

"No game. I have information about Rinehart, but I have other information, too. The first you can get pretty cheap. Five hundred bucks, and I'll give you a list of Rinehart's friends and the people he was hanging with this past month. Ten thousand, and I'll give you the rest of what I know."

Ten thousand dollars?

That was an astronomical amount. Not something a Sagebrush snitch would ever think to ask for. Unless he had something bigger than big to share. The thought made the hair on the back of Austin's neck stand on end.

"Five hundred is steep. I'll give you three, and the list better be complete." He kept his tone even as he responded. No sense in letting Keevers know that he was interested.

"What about the rest?"

"There isn't much I can think of that would be worth ten thousand dollars, Pauly."

"This will be. I guarantee it."

"I'll have to check with my captain."

"You go ahead and do that, Detective, but the longer you wait, the higher the price goes."

"And the more annoyed you make me, the lower your payday for the list of Rinehart's friends will be. We're at three hundred now. In another ten seconds, we'll be down to two-fifty."

"Now, wait a minute—"

"I can get the names myself. We both know it. Maybe it will take a little more time and energy, but it might be worth it so that I don't have to deal with you."

"I'm wounded, Detective." Keevers laughed again, and Austin thought about hanging up on him. His curiosity wouldn't let him. Keevers might be a bad guy, but he had a reputation for selling the truth.

"Not as much as you will be if you waste my time. I'm going to have to go to a lot of trouble to get the kind of money you're asking for."

"It won't be a waste of effort. I can tell you that."

"We'll see. Meet me at the west entrance of

the Lost Woods at noon tomorrow. I'll bring the money for the information about Rinehart and the answer about the rest from my captain. You bring the list. We'll discuss the terms of our next deal then." He hung up on Pauly's sputtered protest.

He'd show. Pauly was nothing if not greedy and eager for a quick buck.

But ten thousand dollars was way more than he'd ever asked for before.

He dialed Slade's number, waiting impatiently while the phone rang. Once. Twice. Three times.

"Slade here."

"It's Austin."

"You're at the prison already?"

"Yes, but I haven't been in yet. I just got off the phone with Pauly Keevers."

"What kind of information does he have to offer? It better be good or he's not getting a dime," Slade growled, his voice gritty and a little worn.

"You okay, Slade?"

"Just tired of hearing the same thing from the doctors. No improvement. You'd think with modern medicine being what it is, they'd be able to bring someone out of a coma."

"You're at the hospital with your dad?"

"Yeah. Hold on. The nurse just walked in."

Austin waited, listening to the faint conversation, his fingers tapping his thigh, his gaze on the brick facade of the prison. Camden West was somewhere on the other side of that wall, and Austin was anxious to pick the guy's brains.

"I'm back. Sorry about that," Slade said.

"No problem."

"Tell me about Keevers."

"He says he has some big information to share. He wants ten thousand dollars for it."

Slade whistled softly. "That's a lot of money."

"Exactly."

"Did he say what kind of information it is?"

"You know Pauly. He was vague and slightly full of his own importance."

"We can't pay that kind of money if we don't know what we're paying for."

"I set up a meeting with him for tomorrow. He's going to bring me a list of Rinehart's associates."

"How much for that?" Slade asked.

"Three hundred."

"Good. You pay him that. Ask for more information about the other. He's not getting another cent until he tells us what we're paying for. Pass that message along for me, and let's see what Keevers says."

"Will do." Austin disconnected and jumped out of the SUV. Time to interview Camden. See what Rinehart's good friend had to say.

Twenty minutes later, he realized Camden wasn't going to say anything at all. He stared into the man's pockmarked face, tried to read something in his blank eyes and dead expression.

"You're telling me that you don't know anything about who Rinehart was hanging with in the weeks before his death?"

"Said it ten times already, Detective. Not going to change my story to make you happy."

"You might want to change it to make yourself happy, Camden. Rinehart is dead. His folks are going to bury him next week."

Camden flinched at the words. A chink in his armor, and Austin was ready to hammer into it, see if he could break him down.

"Here's the deal. Nothing you tell me about your old friend can hurt him, but it might help you. The way I hear it, you're wanting work privileges. You help me out, and I might be able to help you."

Camden's eyes widened, but he didn't take the bait. "I told you that I don't know nothin'."

"You're lying. You know something. You and Rinehart grew up together. You were like brothers. You shared booze and drugs. You can't tell me that he didn't let you in on his secrets."

"You're right. We were like brothers, but that doesn't mean I know all his business." His gaze skirted away.

"You know it all, and you know who he was

working for when he died. Are you going to let his killer go unpunished?"

"The way I hear it, you pulled the trigger. Doesn't that make you his killer?"

"I pulled the trigger, but the person who paid your friend to steal a police captain's dog and kidnap a seven-year-old is responsible for Jeb's death."

"Let's say I agree. Let's even say that you're right. Me and Jeb were like blood, and I want to do right by him." Camden leaned in close, his eyes yellow flecked with brown, his breath reeking of onion and old food as he whispered, "But I got a wife and two kids. Another few months, and I'm up for parole. I want to go home to them. Not be buried ten feet under and never seen again."

Austin's pulse jumped at his words, at the fear in his eyes. "We can offer protection if you need it."

"No one can offer that. Not for me. Not for my family. Not if I talk, and I'm not going to."

"Tell me what you know, Camden. I promise you, I'll put in a good word with the parole board, and I'll make sure your wife and kids are safe until you're released. As soon as you're out, we'll relocate your family. Set you up in a nice little house, help you start a new life." Austin sweetened the pot, sure that Camden wouldn't be able to resist.

"You ask me about anything else and I'll talk, but I'm not talking about the guy who hired Jeb. Sorry, Detective. I'm done." He stood and shuffled to the door, motioned for the guard who stood on the other side.

Austin nodded, and the guard opened the door, led Camden away.

The interview hadn't gone the way he'd hoped, but Austin had learned something. Someone *had* hired Rinehart, and whoever it was had the ability to terrify hardened criminals.

The Boss?

The more Austin learned, the more convinced he became that there was a puppet master pulling strings in Sagebrush.

Who?

Why?

He had to find out if he was ever going to close the case and bring Rio home to Slade and Caleb. Had to solve it if he was going to protect Brady.

And he was. He had no other choice.

Slade was his boss, his friend, a man he respected and admired. He couldn't fail him.

He couldn't fail Eva and Brady, either. As much as he had wanted to stay emotionally distant, as many times as he'd reminded himself that he shouldn't get too involved, he'd already broken every rule he'd made for himself. Already fallen into the depth of Eva's eyes, looked into Brady's

face and seen a child who needed him. A dangerous thing, but he couldn't seem to back off from
it. Couldn't seem to change direction.

Wasn't even sure that he was supposed to.

God's plan. Not his. That's what Austin had
always wanted. What he'd sought every day for
years. Sometimes it was difficult to know where
his will ended and God's began, to find that place
where his desire to control things, to make things
happen was superseded by the knowledge that
God was the master planner, the creator of every
opportunity.

He sighed and pulled away from the prison, his
thoughts swirling like mist on a lake. The truth
was that, aside from his work, he didn't know
where his life was heading. Didn't know what
direction he was going. Only knew that eventually God would lead him to the place he was supposed to be.

TWELVE

"Can I go outside, Momma? *Please?*" Brady's wheedling tone drilled its way into Eva's skull and settled there, pounding behind her eyes and in the base of her neck. She popped the lid on a bottle of aspirin before she answered, swallowing two pills down with a gulp of cold, black coffee.

Patience.

She needed it.

Two days trapped in the house with her grumpy son, and she'd had about all she could take of him and of herself.

"Brady, you know that the doctor said you need to rest for the next few days. Resting doesn't mean going outside in the cold." She kept her tone light despite the fact that she'd answered the same question a half a dozen times.

"It's not cold. The sun is even out." Brady pressed his face to the living-room window, the scratches on his cheek and the bruise on his forehead stark reminders of his reasons for being grouchy. He hadn't slept well in the hospital. Wasn't sleeping well at home. Eva wanted to change that, but no amount of comforting words seemed to help.

"Forty degrees is cold, and that's what the thermometer on the back deck says the temperature is."

"Can I go look?"

"You know you can't."

"But—"

"No more arguing."

"Okay. I guess I'll just play with my Legos." He sighed dramatically and went to the plastic bin he'd left on the coffee table. He dumped the bin on the floor, sorting through the blocks with such intense concentration, Eva smiled.

"What are you going to build?"

"A doghouse."

"For Lightning?" She looked at the big, white stuffed dog that Arianna had given him.

"For Justice. When Austin brings him over—"

"They might not have time to stop by today. You know that, right?" It had been a full day since they'd heard from Austin, and Eva wasn't disappointed about that.

Much.

She frowned, rubbing the knot in the back of her neck.

She wasn't disappointed *at all*.

As a matter of fact, she was relieved.

The last thing she needed was one more complication in her already complicated life. She glanced at the flashing light on the answering machine. Dozens of friends had called since Brady's release from the hospital. So many that she'd begun screening her calls and letting most go to voice mail. She appreciated her friend's concern, but she and Brady both needed some quiet time if they were ever going to begin to heal.

"They will come, Momma. Austin said they would."

"Sometimes things come up. Emergency things."

"Austin will come," he insisted.

"Right. It's lunchtime. How about we make some macaroni?"

"I'm still building my doghouse. Hey, you know what?"

"What?"

"If Justice can't fit in it, we can use it when we get our puppy."

"I never said we were going to get a puppy."

"But you like Justice. We could get one just like him."

"Sweetie—"

"I'd take care of him. I'd feed him and take him for walks—"

The doorbell rang and he jumped up, nearly stumbling in his haste to get to the door.

Eva pulled him up short. "Wait."

"It's Austin. I know it is!"

"We always look before we open the door." She glanced through the peephole, saw Daniel Heppner standing on the porch. Letter carrier and a deacon at Eva's church, he'd been working the same route for three decades, his grizzled face and bright smile a comforting sight.

So why did she feel slightly disappointed?

She opened the door. "Daniel! How are you?"

"I was just going to ask you the same thing. Quite a to-do you've had around here."

"It's definitely been a long couple of days."

"Sounds like it. I couldn't believe it when I saw the story on the news the night Brady was kidnapped. Went out to the woods and joined one of them search parties."

"That means the world to me, Daniel."

"Shouldn't. We didn't find him. You and that detective did that all by yourselves."

"It was Austin's dog who found me. Justice is the best dog ever!" Brady exclaimed, and Daniel smiled down at the boy.

"A bloodhound, right? Saw him on the news, too. You know, when I was your age, I had myself a bloodhound. Me and my dad used to use him for hunting. Name was Mule 'cause he was a stubborn old dog, but I sure did love him."

"Momma is thinking about letting me get a bloodhound in the summer."

"I never said that, Brady."

"Every boy needs a dog, Eva, and a bloodhound is as good a dog as any."

"See, Momma?" Brady beamed, and Eva didn't have the heart to tell him to forget his dream. What was the harm in it? Besides, maybe they would get a puppy in the summer. A little bloodhound with Justice's hangdog face.

"We'll talk about it."

"That's good news, young man. When a mother is open to talking, it means she's almost convinced. Now, I've got to give you what I came with and get back to my route." He held a package out to Brady.

"It's for me?"

"Your name is right on it, son, and I don't know any other Brady Billows."

"Thanks!" Brady took it. "Can I open it, Momma?"

"After Daniel leaves." She took the package from her son's hands, frowning at Brady's name scribbled across white wrapping paper. "I wonder who it's from."

"Can't say, but I can tell you that it was sent overnight from San Antonio yesterday."

"Strange. We don't know anyone from there."

"Lots of people know you, though. At least they know of you and your son. Stories have been running on the news all over Texas. Even had a cousin in Houston call to ask if I knew your boy. Wanted to know how he could pray for you." He glanced at his watch. "Now, I really do have to be on my way. It's me and Agatha's thirty-fifth anniversary, and if I'm late for lunch, it might be our last."

"I don't think she'll kick you to the curb for being a few minutes later." Eva laughed.

"Not when she sees the diamond ring I bought her. Seeing as how she's put up with me for so long, I figured she deserved it. Hope she likes it. Took me nearly a month to find the perfect one."

"She's going to love it." Eva smiled, her heart giving a little twinge of longing. She'd once dreamed of having the kind of relationship that Daniel and his wife had. She'd thought she could find someone she could love wholeheartedly and who would love her the same way. A friend, a lover, an ally during the good times and the bad. When Rick had walked into Arianna's Café, smiled into her eyes and told her she was the most beautiful woman he'd ever seen, she was sure that he was the answer to those dreams.

She couldn't have been more wrong.

"You make sure you ask her about the ring on Sunday, okay? She'll want to show it off. One carat of sparkling diamond and a pretty gold band. Of course, it can't compare to the beauty of the woman who will be wearing it." Daniel winked, and the little ache of longing in Eva's heart became a full-blown throb. "Enjoy your package, little Brady. See you tomorrow!"

"See you, Big Daniel," Brady replied.

Eva closed the front door, slid the bolt home and carried the package into the kitchen, studying the scrawled name and address for several minutes. Nothing out of the ordinary except that she and Brady didn't get packages in the mail; they had no family or friends in San Antonio and...

Nothing.

But unease snaked its way around her heart and squeezed tight.

"Can I open it, Momma?" Brady reached for the package.

"Not yet," she said, grabbing his hand, reluctant to even have him touch it.

"But Daniel said it's for me."

"It's addressed to you, that's for sure, but we don't know who it's from."

"Maybe they put a note in the box."

"Maybe."

"If we open it, we'll know."

"Right." She held the box to her ear, feeling like a fool, but unable to make herself remove the tape that held the paper in place.

"What are you trying to hear?"

"Nothing. I'm just being silly." She pulled at

the tape, slowly peeling back the paper and revealing a shoe box.

Nothing remarkable about that.

The lid was taped closed, and she slid her finger under the edge, ran her fingernail through one piece, her heart racing, her mouth dry with fear.

Over a shoe box wrapped in white paper.

"Is it shoes?" Brady edged in closer as she cut through another piece of tape.

"If it is, they're not your size." She slid her fingernail through a third piece of tape, and Brady frowned.

"The bottom of the box is all messy, Momma."

"Is it? She turned the box, saw an oily stain there.

"Do you think there's food in it?"

"I don't know, but I think maybe we should have that police officer who's sitting outside come in and take a look."

"Why? Do you think there's something bad in there?" Brady's eyes widened, and he stepped back.

"Not really." But she could not make herself break through the last few pieces of tape and remove the lid. "Come on. You can work on that doghouse while the police officer checks things out."

She led Brady into the living room and opened the front door.

* * *

"One. Two. Three." Austin slapped the hundred-dollar bills into Pauly Keevers's hand, doing his best to avoid looking into the snitch's triumphant face. If he looked too long, he might be tempted to do something he'd regret. Like shove a fist into Pauly's smiling mouth. Much as he wanted the information, he hated using a criminal to get it.

"Pleasure doing business with you, Detective." Pauly's gleeful tone did nothing to improve Austin's mood.

"I wish I could say the same."

"I guess you being a police officer makes it tough to pay a guy like me. Think of it this way, though. You got what you needed and saved the city time and money in the process."

"Always a businessman. Right, Pauly?"

"Exactly. And if you think about it even more, you might even agree that we're in the same business. We both bring bad guys down. I just happen to—"

"Be one of them?"

Pauly's laughter scared several blackbirds from a nearby tree. "Man, you kill me, Detective! Now, you've got your information, and I've got a little spending money. I guess it's time to say goodbye."

"Not so fast." Austin grabbed Pauly's arm. "You said you had some other information for sale."

"I changed my mind."

"Too bad. My captain says we may be willing to pay. It all depends on the information."

"Like I said. I changed my mind," Pauly insisted, but there was no mistaking the hunger in his eyes. The greed. It gleamed dark and sharp, and Austin had every intention of taking advantage of it.

"Ten thousand is a lot of cash, Pauly. Way more than the three hundred you're clutching."

"True." Pauly glanced at the three bills and frowned.

"A guy like you could do a lot with ten thousand dollars, and it's not like anyone would know that you were the one who provided the information." Austin pressed the advantage, Pauly's reluctance making him more interested than ever in finding out what he had to offer.

"You know how to make a guy think, that's for sure. But there's only one thing I like more than money."

"What's that?"

"Me."

"You're scared." Not a question, but Pauly sniffed, his dark eyes flashing.

"Cautious. So how about you give me a little time to decide how much information I want to share? I'll get back to you in a few days."

"Sorry. We either do the deal now, or we don't do it at all."

Pauly scowled, but he didn't refuse. "Tell you what. I'll give the captain something to think about. After we've all had some time to mull things over, I'll give you a call. Just warning you, though. *If* I decide to talk, it's going to cost a couple of thousand more than the price I already named."

"You're getting greedy, Pauly."

"I've always been greedy." Keevers grinned, but his shoulders were tense, his hands fisted.

"What do you want me to tell the captain?"

"You tell him there's been stuff going on in Sagebrush for years. Little things, but they're all connected to something way bigger."

"That's too vague. Give me something more or the deal's off."

"We haven't agreed to a deal, Detective," Pauly said, but the bait had been set, and he was already in the trap. They both knew it. Keevers might love himself, but he would never turn down the kind of money that they were talking about.

"Enjoy your three hundred, Pauly." Austin started walking away, knowing before the other man called out that he would.

"You want to give him something to really sink his teeth into? Tell him that the Billows murder, the two bank heists last year and the O'Reilly missing-persons case are all related," Pauly said as Austin opened the door of the SUV.

"You have proof of that?" Austin knew about the cases Pauly was referring to. He'd actually worked the O'Reilly case. A high school football coach who'd been accused of dealing drugs, Mitch O'Reilly had disappeared two days before he was scheduled to appear in court. Austin and Justice had been called in, but they'd never found the coach or his body.

"I've heard talk."

"From who?"

"I can't tell you that, Detective. Bad for business. As for proof, that's more your expertise than mine."

"We're not paying ten thousand for speculation." Austin's cell phone rang. He ignored it. Didn't want to lose the thread of the conversation or give Keevers a reason to walk away.

Pauly shrugged, his eyes filled with hunger again, his gaze sharp and just slightly amused. "You asked for a list of Jeb Rinehart's recent associates. You've got it. Now I'm heading out. I've got things to do. Money to spend. I'll give you a call when I have time."

"Give me a call in the next twenty-four hours or don't bother calling at all."

"I'll keep that in mind." Pauly swaggered away, and Austin let him, his mind humming with possibilities. He was on the scent of something big, and he didn't want to let it go. Wouldn't let it go. First, Brady's information about The Boss. Now, Pauly's assertion that several major crimes were connected.

A puppet master pulling strings.

He'd thought it before.

Knew it now.

All he had to do was find exactly what he'd told Keevers that he needed—proof.

He checked his cell phone as he climbed into the SUV, frowning as he read Captain McNeal's number.

He hit redial, waiting impatiently while the phone rang.

"It's about time," Slade growled.

"I was in the middle of my meeting with Keevers. What's up?"

"I just arrived at the Billows's house. Jackson and Titan have been called in."

"A bomb?" There'd be no reason to call in Jackson and his black lab otherwise, and Austin's blood ran cold at the thought.

"We're not sure. Brady received a package in the mail. Something about it made Eva nervous. She called in the patrol officer who's outside her house. He was concerned enough to call dispatch and ask for backup."

"I'm on my way." He sped from the entrance of

the woods, branches of low-hanging trees brushing the top of the SUV as it bounced over the rutted road. Justice whined impatiently, sensing Austin's tension and adrenaline. Probably hoping they were going to work.

"Sorry, boy, it's Titan's turn," he said, keeping his tone easy and neutral. Justice picked up on body language and vocal cues, and Austin kept that in mind when working with the bloodhound. Still, he couldn't control his body's reaction to stress, his rapid heartbeat and wildly racing pulse. After the kidnapping, they'd been expecting another overt attempt on Brady's life and had planned accordingly. Police patrol. Twenty-four-hour guard.

It hadn't been enough.

Brady could have died.

Eva could have, as well.

He scowled, pressing on the gas and shooting onto the highway, sirens blaring, nerves humming, everything inside shouting for him to hurry.

It took twenty minutes to get to Eva's neighborhood. Oak Street had been cordoned off, and a patrol officer checked Austin's ID and waved him through the barricade.

Several police cars were parked in Eva's driveway, and curious neighbors stood in a yard three houses up.

Austin grabbed Justice's leash and opened the hatchback. "Want to go visit Brady?"

Justice whined, his nose twitching with enthusiasm as he jumped to the pavement. No orange vest, so he knew he wasn't on the job, but he seemed to recognize Eva's house, his tail wagging rapidly as they walked up the porch stairs.

"I'm glad you made it, Austin. The captain has been asking for you." Valerie walked toward him, her coppery-red hair in a high ponytail, her uniform pressed and crisp.

"I got here as quickly as I could. Any response from Titan?"

"He alerted. Slade called in the bomb squad and escorted the Billowses to his place. He should be back in a couple of minutes. I'm clearing the block. You want to give me a hand?"

"Sure." But what he really wanted to do was head over to Slade's, make sure that Eva and Brady were okay.

"Thanks. I'll take the east end of the street. You handle the west," Eva suggested.

"What about Jackson? Is he still inside?"

"He's already gone back to the station. He's calling San Antonio P.D. Wants to see if they'll send a man out to the post office that the package was mailed from. The Feds will be involved, too, of course. We'd better get moving. The captain wants these houses cleared before the bomb squad arrives." Valerie smoothed a hand over her hair and shoved her hat back on as she hurried toward a group huddled in a neighbor's yard.

Austin led Justice in the opposite direction, the truth of what had almost happened pulsing through his blood. A bomb mailed to a seven-year-old child? What kind of person did something like that? Then again, what kind of person climbed into a kid's window during the dead of night and kidnapped him? Not the kind Austin wanted out on the street. That was for sure.

He'd already been feeling the pressure of time passing, the quick tick of the clock marking the minutes since Rio was stolen and Brady kidnapped. It seemed louder now, the beat of his heart echoing the passing moments, reminding him that each second that went by without a perp in jail was another second that Brady remained in danger and that Slade and his son remained separated from the German shepherd that they considered part of their family.

He knocked on the door of Eva's neighbor, his gaze flickering to a spot up the street. Slade's house. Eva and Brady tucked safely away inside of it.

Only no one could be safe if bombs were being used.

Explosives could destroy houses, buildings, cars.

Take out an entire block if enough of them were used.

"Yes?" The door opened a couple of inches, and he turned his attention to the elderly woman who peered out from the crack in the door, her blue eyes wide behind thick lenses.

"Detective Austin Black with the Sagebrush Police Department. Are you the only one home?" he asked as he flashed his badge and tried to refocus his energy and thoughts.

He *would* find the person responsible for the bomb.

First, though, he needed to clear the block.

THIRTEEN

A bomb.

A real bomb that could have exploded. One that might have killed Brady. The thought made Eva dizzy, terrified her in the same guttural way that finding Brady's empty bed had.

She paced Slade's living room, wishing that she could grab Brady, get in her old, battered station wagon and drive until they reached a place where no one knew them.

The problem was, she didn't know how far she'd have to go to outrun the danger that seemed to be stalking her son. A hundred miles? A thousand?

"Eva, why don't you sit down? Pacing isn't going to change things." The police captain set a large plastic bin filled with cars in front of Brady. "These are Caleb's. I'm sure that he won't mind if you play with them."

"Thank you," Brady said, his eyes wide with surprise and awe. He had toys, but not large bins full. Eva didn't have the money for them. Most days that didn't bother her. Today, watching Brady dig through the toy cars, Slade's retired K-9 partner lying beside him, his head on Brady's leg, it made her heart ache.

"No problem. Now, if you two will excuse me. I've got to get back to your place. Officer Lawrence will stay with you until I get back."

"What about Austin? Can't he stay with us?" Brady asked, looking up from a car he was rolling along the floor.

"Austin should be arriving shortly. I'll ask him to stop in when he has time." If Slade was surprised by Brady's request, it didn't show. He just grabbed his coat and nodded to the taciturn officer who stood near his front door. Average height and build with flashing black eyes and a fierce scowl, he looked about as happy to be standing guard as Eva was to be pacing Slade's living room.

Someone tapped on the front door, and it swung open. Crisp air tinged with rain drifted in as Austin stepped into the room with Justice.

Austin.

Eva hadn't known that she'd been waiting for him until he appeared. Hadn't known how much she'd craved having him near until he walked toward her.

"Austin! Justice!" Brady jumped up, flung himself at Austin's knees.

"Brady, don't." She tried to dislodge him, but Austin brushed her hands away.

"It's okay. We're buddies, right, sport?"

"Yes. Guess what?"

"What?"

"There's a bomb at my house." Brady sounded fascinated and terrified, and Austin must have heard both in his voice. He crouched so they were eye to eye.

"I heard about that. There are people over at your place taking care of it. When you go home, you don't have to worry about it anymore."

"Maybe someone is going to send me another one."

"If someone does, your mom will call for help again. Just like she did this time." He straightened, his attention on Slade. "The bomb squad just arrived."

"Good. I'm heading back over. You want to come with me or stay here?"

"I'll stay."

"Put yourself to good use and interview the witnesses, will you? I'm leaving Officer Lawrence as extra insurance. We can't afford to lose our primary witness."

Primary witness?

Brady was more than that, and Eva wanted to say it. Wanted to tell Slade what he could do with his extra insurance and his house and his son's bucket of cars.

She kept her silence as he walked outside. Kept it as he closed the door. Kept it because it wasn't his fault that her life had fallen to pieces.

"Get any hotter and steam is going to start pouring out of your ears," Austin murmured, his lips brushing her hair as he steered her to the sofa. "Sit. You're pale as paper."

"I'm naturally fair." But her migraine was back and her stomach was sick, and every time she thought about the package that she'd almost opened, her knees went weak.

She collapsed onto a nicely cushioned sofa. So much better than the Goodwill store special that she'd bought the day she'd signed the mortgage on her little house. She tamped down envy, reminded herself that she was working toward her goals. That before she knew it, she'd have her degree and the job she wanted somewhere far away from Sagebrush and all its horrible memories.

"Are you doing okay?" Austin sat beside her, his scent wrapping her up in warmth and comfort and familiarity. Although she'd only known him for a few days, it felt like she'd known him for a lifetime.

Terrifying.

So was the look in his eyes, the depth of his

gaze. The way looking at him felt like looking at every dream she'd ever had.

"I'm fine."

"You don't look fine," he said quietly.

"How is someone supposed to look after a bomb is mailed to her son?" She focused her attention on Brady, on Officer Lawrence, on the floor. On everything and anything but Austin.

"Probably a whole lot like you. About ready to fall over," he responded, and she couldn't help smiling, couldn't stop herself from looking right into his handsome face.

Big mistake.

Her heart throbbed, her breath caught.

Pull yourself together. He's just a man.

Right. *Just* a man.

One who'd acted like a hero and who treated her son like he mattered and who Eva could almost believe in.

Almost.

"Don't worry. I'm not planning to collapse."

"Glad to hear it. Much as I'd like to sweep you off your feet, I'm not sure either of us would want me to have to sweep you up off the floor."

"Neither of those things is going to happen."

"We'll see. Do you mind if I ask Brady a few questions?" He changed the subject, and she let him, because trying to continue it would make it seem as if she cared one way or another.

She didn't.

Shouldn't.

But maybe the thought of being swept off her feet wasn't quite as awful as it had been a week ago. Especially if the person doing the sweeping was Austin.

"He's really shaken. It might be better for him if you waited." And better for *her* if Austin left.

"Then I guess we can get started on your interview. How about we go in the kitchen?" He pulled her to her feet, and a million butterflies took flight in her stomach.

"I'd rather not leave Brady alone."

"I'm not alone, Momma. Justice is with me," Brady said as he rolled a police car in front of the bloodhound's nose. The dog sniffed it, licked Brady's cheek and settled into a heap of fur beside him.

"I know, sweetie, but—"

"He'll be fine, ma'am. I'm here to keep an eye on him," Officer Lawrence said, speaking up for the first time since he'd arrived.

Not the best timing, in Eva's opinion.

"Right. I guess it's fine, then."

"Great. This shouldn't take more than a few minutes." Austin pressed a hand to her lower back, his palm burning through her T-shirt, the heat seeping through her skin and into her blood, burning her cheeks and her heart.

She felt like a schoolgirl with her first crush. Only she wasn't a girl, and she knew exactly where crushes could lead.

"Go ahead and have a seat." Austin gestured to the dinette set that sat in a corner of the room, and she perched on the edge of a chair.

"You've got a little color back in your cheeks. Feeling better?" Austin dropped into the chair across from Eva, studying her face as she quickly braided her hair and unbraided it again, the silky gold strands sliding through her fingers.

She seemed fidgety and tense, her gaze skittering away from his, her foot tapping on the tile floor. "I'm not sure there's much that I can tell you, Austin. The box was delivered by our regular mail carrier, and I know that he'd never hurt Brady."

"It was postmarked San Antonio, so we've got no reason to believe it didn't come from there. I'm curious as to what made you suspicious of it, though."

"I already told Officer Lawrence—the bottom of the box was seeping something. That seemed odd. Plus, I don't know anyone in San Antonio." She drummed the table with her fingertips, still not meeting his eyes.

"You don't have to be nervous around me, Eva." He covered her hand, and she stilled, her gaze finally settling on him.

"I'm not."

He quirked a brow. "Then why all the fidgeting?"

"I have a lot of energy?"

"Nice try, but I'm not buying it. Want to try the truth, instead?"

"Sure. Why not? Here's the thing, Austin. I've been swept off my feet before, and I don't want to be again." She sighed, pressing her fingers to the bridge of her nose and closing her eyes briefly. When she opened them, he was struck again by their beauty, the soft green mistiness of them, the quiet stillness in their depths.

"My comment about sweeping you off your feet was a joke, Eva."

"Was it?" she asked, and he couldn't give her anything but the truth.

"Yes, but there might have been a grain of truth in it."

"Austin—"

"You're a beautiful, intelligent woman and you're a wonderful mother. That combination is hard to resist."

"Yeah. I've been fighting men off for years." She smiled, walked to the window that looked out over Slade's backyard.

"Then you know that no one can sweep you off your feet unless you want to be swept."

"I was kidding about fighting men off. It's just

been me and Brady since the day he was born. That's the way I've wanted it."

"Is it the way you still want it?" he asked softly.

"I…don't want to get hurt again. That's what I know. I don't want Brady to be hurt. He's a little boy with big dreams and a wide-open heart. I want him to stay that way for as long as he can."

"You can't protect him from hurt, Eva. It's part of life. You can't make your childhood better by making his perfect, either."

"I'm not trying to. I'm just trying to give him the best possible life he can have. I'm trying to make sure he has the kind of love and security I didn't. There's nothing wrong with that."

"I never said that there was. I'm just saying that you can't give up your possibilities because you're afraid of what will happen to Brady if you go after them. As long as he has your love, he'll be just fine." He urged her around so they were facing each other. Tears glittered in her eyes, but they didn't fall, and he wondered if she ever cried, ever allowed herself to feel whatever it was that simmered in the depth of her gaze.

"I thought you needed to ask me some questions." She moved away, sat at the table again, her face pinched and hollow.

"Has Brady been talking about the kidnapping?" If she wanted to change the subject, he'd comply, but they weren't finished with the conversation. Not by a long shot.

There was something about Eva that called to him, some part of her heart that seemed made for his. He couldn't deny that any more than he could allow himself to push for something she didn't seem to want.

"No. I think he's been trying to forget it. Maybe even pretend it didn't happen. Then the package came, and he's right back where he was a couple of days ago—terrified."

"I'm sorry for that, Eva. I wish I could make it all go away, but I can't."

"You're a hero, but not a superhero, huh?" she said, and blushed.

"I don't have a cape tucked away in my backpack that I can take out and use when I need to swoop in and rescue my friends, that's for sure."

"Too bad. If you did, you could break out the cape, and Brady and I could hitch a ride out of town."

He met her eyes. "You're thinking of leaving?"

"Just thinking that it might be safer to go than to stay."

"Go where?"

"I don't know. I could drive east or head north. I'm sure that we could find a nice quiet little town to hole up in."

"You know that won't protect Brady, Eva," he

reminded her. "It'll just take you both away from the people who want to help you."

"Maybe, but I just want so badly for him to be safe."

"He will be. I promise you that."

A shadow crossed her face. "Don't make me promises, okay, Austin? Everyone who ever has just ended up disappointing me."

"Then they were all too foolish to know what they'd be losing out on when you walked away."

"And you're not?"

"I guess that will be up to you to decide," he responded, lifting her hand, his thumb trailing over her red and cracked knuckles.

For a moment, Eva went perfectly still, her eyes wide with surprise.

"I—" She stood, nearly toppling the chair in her haste. "If we're done, I think I'd better go check on Brady," she said, and then she ran from the room.

Eva figured that she could run from the room, the house, the town, the country, but there was no way she could run from the way Austin made her feel. His words were still echoing in her head as she plopped down beside Brady, scratched Justice's silky ears and tried her best to quiet her rioting heart.

"Are you okay, Momma? Your cheeks are all red," Brady said, his big, blue eyes shadowed with anxiety. With everything else that had happened, he didn't need anything more to worry about, and she hugged him close, pressed a gentle kiss to his bruised forehead.

"I'm fine."

"Then why are your cheeks red?"

"Because—"

The front door opened, and Slade walked into the house, his dark hair mussed, his expression grim. "The bomb squad is finished. An evidence team is over at your place, but I think it's safe for you and Brady to go home."

"Did they detonate the explosives?" Austin asked as he strode out of the kitchen. The question was for Slade, but his gaze was on Eva.

"Yes. The bomb was rudimentary at best. Probably put together by someone who downloaded instructions off the internet."

"Then it wouldn't have done much damage?" It's what Eva wanted to believe, but Slade shook his head.

"It might have been rudimentary, but it still would have done plenty of damage. Come on... I'll walk you two home. What time does your shift end, Officer Lawrence?"

"Another hour."

"You want to accompany us, then?"

"Sure. I'll wait outside until you're ready." The officer stepped outside, the door closing softly behind him.

"Why don't you let me escort them, Slade? I'm parked over there, anyway," Austin offered.

"Sounds good. When you're done, I'd like you to come to the station. I'm calling a meeting of the K-9 Unit. We need to discuss what you found out from West and Keevers, and we may as well do it as a group," Slade said.

Too bad, because spending more time with Austin wasn't something Eva should be doing. Not if she wanted to guard her heart.

"Let's get those cars cleaned up, Brady," she said, tossing a handful of cars into the bin, her cheeks still too hot, her heart still beating wildly.

"I'll give you a hand."

Austin. Of course.

His shoulder brushed hers as they worked, his scent masculine and compelling.

"Done!" She threw the last car in the bin, grabbed Brady's hand. "Let's go."

"Are we in a hurry?" Austin asked, opening the door and letting her step out ahead of him.

"I'm just anxious to get home."

"Tired?"

She sighed. "It's been a rough couple of days."

"Things will get better." He shortened Justice's leash. "Hey, sport, you want to help me walk Justice back to your house?"

"Really? Sure!" Brady's smile looked like Christmas morning and birthday presents all rolled into one.

"Put your hand here." He helped Brady slide his hand through the loop in the leash, and Eva's heart melted into a puddle of longing so deep she thought she might drown in it.

This was what Brady had been missing.

What he probably hadn't even known he'd wanted until Austin had walked into their lives.

What would happen when he walked out?

"I wish you wouldn't—" she started to say, but couldn't finish. Couldn't deny Brady a few minutes of excitement because of her own insecurities and fears.

"What?"

"Nothing important."

"Good." Austin grinned, urging her up the street.

She could feel the weight of a dozen eyes. Her neighbors, watching as the good-looking police detective escorted her home. No matter that another officer was a few feet ahead of them, never mind that a bomb had been discovered in a package addressed to Brady. In their minds, they'd have her married off to Austin by the next morning, and there wasn't a whole lot she could do about it.

"Keep frowning like that and you'll have wrinkles before you're thirty," Austin chided as they walked up her porch stairs. Crime-scene tape dangled from the railing and flapped in the cold breeze.

"A gentleman wouldn't mention such a thing."

"Who said that I'm a gentleman?" He took the leash from Brady's hand, ruffled his hair. "Thanks for the help, sport. I'll see you later."

Don't tell him that, she wanted to say. *Don't lead him on and disappoint him.*

But Austin touched her cheek, his fingers gentle as a butterfly's kiss. "See you later, too."

She heard the promise in his voice, saw it in his eyes, and she couldn't find it in herself to say anything at all.

FOURTEEN

Austin had never been big on meetings. He preferred action to words and would rather be out following a scent trail with Justice than sitting in a conference room sipping coffee and listening to the team discuss the details of a case. A necessary evil, that's how he thought of them. Today, though, he was hoping that the meeting would turn out to be way more than that.

Things were escalating, the bomb an indication that the person who'd kidnapped Brady was getting desperate. That desperation could only lead to more aggressive attempts on Brady's life. The Special Operations K-9 Unit needed to shut the guy down and lock him up before that could happen.

Guy?

Guy*s*.

The brown-haired kidnapper and The Boss.

Austin snagged a cookie from a plate someone had set in the middle of the long table and bit into it as Slade McNeal entered the room and took the seat between Lee Calloway and Parker Adams.

"It looks like we're all here, so I'll go ahead and get started. I have some information to share, and then we'll let Austin and Lee give us their updates." Slade scanned his five member team.

"Information? You mean about the bomb that was mailed to Brady Billows?" Lee Calloway asked.

"We're still working our San Antonio angle, Lee. This has got to be something different," Jackson Worth responded, his dog Titan shifting under Jackson's chair as his handler spoke.

"Right. I got some news a couple of minutes ago, and I'm hoping that it'll help bring this case to a close." McNeal paused. You've heard of Dante Frears? He's an old war buddy of mine."

Austin had heard of him. As a matter of fact, he'd hung out with Slade and Dante on a couple of occasions. A well-respected member of the community, Dante had wealth, power and the kind of good-old-boy charm that had won him friends all over Sagebrush.

"There aren't many people in town who haven't heard of him, Slade. What did he call you about? Does he have information that will help our investigation?" Lee asked.

"Not directly, but he's willing to help us get it. He's offering a twenty-five-thousand-dollar reward to anyone with information that leads to Rio's recovery."

"That's a lot of money," Parker said.

"Hopefully it will be enough to motivate someone to step forward. We need Rio on the force, and I need him home. Caleb isn't doing well with this new loss." Slade didn't talk much about his personal life. The fact that he'd mentioned his five-year-old son hinted at big problems.

"If there's anything I can do to help, let me know. I'm pretty good with kids," Valerie offered.

"Thanks, but the only thing that is going to help Caleb is having Rio back. Now, let's get to our next order of business. Any change with Jane Doe, Lee?"

"She's unconscious, and the doctors don't know how long that will last. Her fingerprints aren't in the system, and so far, no one has reported her missing. Until someone does, we're walking in the dark."

"How about you, Austin? Did your meeting with Camden West pan out?"

"Not even close. He wouldn't talk. Didn't even bite when I mentioned the possibility of early parole and relocation."

"Do you think he's trying to protect someone?" Slade asked.

"I think he's trying to protect himself. He's afraid of someone, and so is Pauly Keevers."

"I find that hard to believe. Word on the street is that Keevers is only afraid of God." Parker leaned back in his chair and frowned.

"I would have said the same about Pauly before I met with him today." Austin filled the team in on his meeting with Keevers.

When he finished, Slade stood and paced to the bank of windows on the far wall. "We've got problems, and they're not limited to Rio's theft. If Keevers's information is accurate and the crimes he mentioned are connected, there's a crime ring in Sagebrush, and it's been operating for years."

Everyone spoke at once after that, a hodgepodge of voices and ideas filling the room. Some members of the team thought Pauly was lying. Others were eager to pay Keevers the money he'd demanded for more information.

Finally, Slade raised his hand, and the group fell silent.

"I'm not sure what we're dealing with, but Pauly has never sold us information that didn't pan out. Austin, when Keevers contacts you again, let him know we're willing to pay what he wants for the information."

Slade left the room and the rest of the team followed, their moods grim. No chatting or joking. With Rio missing, the team felt incomplete, and Slade's concern and anxiety were weighing on everyone.

"Want me to put the word out that you're in the market to buy information again? Get a little fire burning under Keevers?" Parker asked as they walked to their cubicles.

"We're better off waiting. I want Keevers to think he has the upper hand and is calling the shots."

"I hope he wants to call the shots soon, then. Whatever he knows has to be huge if he's worried for his safety."

"Worried or not, I'm hoping he talks," Austin retorted. "If there *is* a crime ring in Sagebrush, I want to take it down."

"I like the way you think, Austin." Parker grinned, but Austin didn't feel much like smiling.

Rio missing. Two victims hospitalized. A little boy in danger. Time ticking away, and Austin had more questions than answers.

He walked into the kennel, retrieved Justice and led him to the SUV. They'd been working long hours, and the bloodhound deserved some time to run and play.

Ten minutes later, he pulled up in front of his two-story Victorian. A pretty house, that's what the women who visited said. The guys couldn't have cared less about the gingerbread trim or the wraparound porch.

Austin cared.

He'd painstakingly restored them. Had done

the same with the interior, refinishing the time-worn hardwood floors and the hand-carved railing that curved up the winding staircase. To Austin each of those things represented everything that he hadn't had when he'd been a kid, moving from low-income apartment to low-income apartment while his mother struggled to provide.

Permanence.

He'd needed it. Now that he had it, he wanted someone to share it with.

He frowned, unlocking the front door and letting Justice run inside ahead of him. If things had worked out with Candace, they might have had a child by now. The house might be filled with the scent of dinner cooking, the sound of a baby crying and the weight of Candace's disappointment.

Yeah.

Things would have been great until he couldn't be there for a birthday party, a dinner date, a movie night.

He pulled a meal from the freezer and shoved it into the microwave, not sure why he was thinking about Candace. He didn't miss her. Didn't wish things had worked out differently.

His cell phone rang and he answered as he took out the meal. "Hello?"

"Austin? It's Eva." She didn't have to tell him. A dozen years from now, he was pretty sure he'd still know exactly what her voice sounded like.

"Is everything okay?"

"Yes. I just…"

"What?" He took a bite of lukewarm pasta and thought that he should invest in some cooking lessons so he could eat better.

"How was your meeting?"

"Interesting. An old friend of Slade's is offering twenty-five-thousand dollars for information leading to Rio's return."

"That's incredible!" She sounded excited, and he smiled, imagining her twisting the end of her long ponytail, her eyes glowing.

"I'm working on a couple of other leads. Nothing I can talk about right now, but I'm hoping we'll be able to find Brady's kidnapper soon."

"Me, too. I'm ready for our lives to go back to normal."

"What's normal for you, Eva? You're a mother, a waitress, a student. What else do you do with your time?"

"Nothing. I don't have time for anything else." She laughed. "What about you? Wait…don't tell me. Let me guess. In your free time, you climb mountains, hike trails and volunteer as a coach for a local football team."

"Not quite." It was his turn to laugh.

"Then what? Aside from convincing little boys that you can almost walk on water, that is."

"Brady doesn't think that."

"No, but he does adore you," she murmured.

"Is that the real reason why you're calling?"

She hesitated. "I just don't want him hurt."

"Why would he be?"

"Because when this is over, you're going to go back to your life, and Brady will be left with his. He may realize how big a hole there is in it."

"What hole?" He shoved his pasta away, looking out into the gray-blue evening.

"He's never had a father. He's never even had a man in his life aside from teachers. That makes the attention you're giving him even more special. Imagine how he'll feel when he doesn't have it anymore."

"You're assuming that he won't," he said, his tone sharper than he'd intended.

"You're upset," she said quietly.

"No. I'm insulted. I like Brady. He's a great kid. I'm not going to track down his kidnapper and then walk out of his life. Not unless you ask me to."

"I—"

"Tell you what. I'm right in the middle of dinner. How about we hash things out later?" He cut her off, not sure he wanted to hear what she had to say. If she told him to back off, he would, but he wouldn't be happy about it.

"What are you having? Anything better than leftover chicken noodle soup?"

"Does overcooked and then frozen pasta count as better?" He nudged a noodle with his fork.

"Tell me you're not really eating that."

"I am. Got it out of my freezer and stuck it in the microwave right before you called."

"That's not healthy eating for a guy who leads such an active life."

"Careful, Eva. Keep talking like that and I might get the impression that you care."

"I never said that I didn't."

"But you don't want to."

"Brady isn't the only one who I think is going to be hurt when this is over." She sighed. "Listen, I've got some cod in the fridge. Why don't you come by, and I'll make it. We can have salad with it, and chocolate chip cookies for dessert."

"Keep tempting me, and I might just take you up on the offer."

"I want you to. I owe you. If it weren't for you and Justice—"

"I don't want your gratitude. If that's what this is about, then I think I'll stick to my pasta."

"I… It's not."

"In that case, what time will dinner be ready?"

"Give me an hour to clean up the kitchen and the rest of the house, then I'll be ready to cook." She hung up, and Austin dumped the pasta into the trash can.

An hour, and he'd be eating dinner with Eva and

Brady, sitting at the table in their little kitchen, feeling like part of something bigger than himself. That's what friendship and family did. They offered a connection that made a single person become something more.

Eva and Brady's faces flashed through his mind.

He could build something with them. He knew it. Build it, nurture it, make it into something better than any of them could have on their own.

He wanted that more than he wanted to be safe.

Wanted it more than he wanted to protect the pieces of his heart.

Prayed that Eva wanted it, too, because finding her and Brady was like finding a puzzle piece that had been missing for far too long.

A perfect fit?

Austin didn't know, but he thought he'd be a fool not find out.

FIFTEEN

She shouldn't have invited him for dinner.

Didn't know why she had.

Or maybe she did.

She liked having Austin around, felt his absence when he was gone.

If Brady was in the throes of hero worship, *she* was in the throes of something far worse.

"Idiot," Eva muttered as she pulled the cod out of the fridge and salted it liberally. She'd pan sear it, serve it with a nice Caesar salad. Feed everyone, and then send Austin away.

Simple as that.

Only nothing seemed simple when Austin was around.

When he was with her, all the promises she'd made to herself, all the things she'd sworn she'd never feel again were right there, telling her that she'd been a fool to ever think she had control over any of them.

The doorbell rang, and Brady shouted excitedly.

"He's here, Momma! Austin is here!"

"I'm coming." She dried her hands on a dish towel, peered out the peephole. She knew who she'd see, but her heart jumped, anyway.

Austin.

She opened the door, stepped back so he and Justice could enter.

"Sorry we're late. We had an errand to run."

"Actually, you're right on time. I was just starting the fish. I'll make the salad after that. We should be able to eat in about fifteen minutes," she said as Brady patted Justice's head. The bloodhound's tongue lolled out in ecstasy, and she was sure there was a smile hidden beneath his jowls.

"Maybe sooner if we use this." Austin pulled a large salad from a brown paper bag. "I thought having it premade might speed up the process."

"You're that hungry?"

"Starving." Austin smiled, his eyes deeply shadowed, his bomber jacket hanging open to reveal a black T-shirt. She wondered what it would be like to lay her head against his chest, hear his heart beating steadily beneath soft cotton and warm flesh.

Stop!

"I'd better get the fish started, then." She turned, and he snagged her belt loop, pulled her back.

"Hold on. I brought something for Brady. I thought you might like to see it, too."

"What?" Presents? She didn't like that, and she thought that she'd have to tell him. Make it clear that she didn't want him to buy her son's affection. It wasn't like he didn't already have it. As a matter of fact…

He pulled a fluffy, white stuffed dog from the bag.

No. Not quite white. The fake fur was a little dingy, but not dirt-encrusted like it had been the last time she'd seen it.

"Snowflake!" Brady took the dog, hugged it to his chest.

"I thought you took that as evidence," Eva said.

"I did, but the forensic team couldn't find anything but mud on it, so I got Slade's permission and signed it out of the evidence room."

"Thank you, Austin! This is the best present ever!" Brady threw himself at Austin, his thin arms wrapping around Austin's broad shoulders. Seeing them together made Eva's heart ache.

She'd always wanted this for Brady. A male influence. Someone her son could look up to. A father figure who could fill the spot that Rick had left. She'd wanted it but had known that going after it could only lead to hurt. Hers *and* Brady's.

So what had she done?

She'd invited Austin for dinner, that's what.

She sighed, heating the pan and laying the fish in it.

"Need any help?" Austin moved up behind her, his chest so close to her back that she could feel his heat through her shirt. She wanted to turn into him, slide her hands up his arms and into his dark hair. Wanted to let herself believe that one moment could lead to another and to another until they'd built hundreds of moments together.

"You can grab some plates from the cupboard." Anything to put some distance between them.

"You're uncomfortable." He opened the cupboard, pulled out three mismatched plates.

"Why do you say that?"

"You're gripping that spatula like you're afraid it's going to jump out of your hand."

"Right." She loosened her grip.

"Momma? Is dinner ready?" Brady padded into the kitchen, Justice right behind him. They looked cute together. The sweet little boy and his furry companion.

Maybe getting a puppy in the summer wasn't such a bad idea.

"Soon. Why don't you help Austin set the table?" She let them work and talk while she finished the fish, plated it and the salad, poured ice water into plastic cups. Did everything the same way she'd done it a thousand times before. Only this time, Austin was there, his gaze following her as she moved around the kitchen, sat in her chair, reached for Brady's hand and for his.

"Do you want to pray, Austin?"

He offered a simple prayer of thanks. Nothing flowery or overwrought. When he was done, he squeezed her hand gently. "This looks good. Thanks for inviting me."

Her cheeks heated at his praise, and she dug into the fish, tried not to think about the fact that they were sitting at her little table together.

Like a family.

Only they weren't.

She finished her fish, but it tasted like sawdust, her heart pounding so frantically she thought she might be sick.

This hadn't just been a bad idea.

It had been a horrible one.

By the time everyone finished eating and she'd tucked Brady into bed, she felt frazzled, her nerves raw.

She poured coffee into two mugs, handed one to Austin, doing her best to avoid his gorgeous eyes.

"What's wrong, Eva?" He took the mug from her hand, cupped her jaw so that she had no choice but to meet his eyes.

"I wish none of this had happened. Not Brady witnessing a crime. Not him being kidnapped. Not the bomb. Not…"

"Us?"

"Is there an us, Austin? Or is this just a game

we're playing until it's over and we find out that we've both lost."

"I don't play games."

"That's what Brady's father told me a couple of days before I found out he was married," she said, and regretted it immediately.

"Let's get one thing straight, okay? I'm not Brady's father, and if I were, I wouldn't be living in Las Vegas while you raised my son," he bit out.

"I know. I'm sorry. I guess that I've just always figured that if I could fall for someone like Rick once, I could do it again."

He searched her eyes. "So you decided not to let yourself fall at all?"

"Something like that."

"How old were you when you met him?" Austin asked.

"Eighteen. He walked into Arianna's Café and started spouting a bunch of pretty phrases. I was convinced he meant them. Convinced that we'd get married and have a beautiful house and beautiful children and live happily ever after. Too bad my Prince Charming turned out to be a toad."

"I'm sorry, Eva. You deserved better."

"My mother said the same thing when I found out that I was pregnant. I think she was relieved that Rick didn't want to leave his wife and make a life with me. She was terrified that I'd end up married to someone just like my father. *You deserve better,* she'd said. Funny that she thought that about me and not about herself."

"Not so funny," he murmured, his hand slipping from her jaw and sliding under the hair at her nape, his palm raspy and warm and altogether too wonderful.

"Austin, this isn't a good idea."

"No?"

"No." But she was leaning into him, her hands on his chest, her fingers curled into the fabric of his shirt, every cell in her body yearning for him in a way that she had never yearned for Rick. Had never yearned for anyone.

"I'll stop if you want me to, Eva. I'll walk away and let you and Brady go on the way you were. Just say the word, and I'll go home."

She couldn't.

Didn't.

And his lips touched hers, gently, easily. No pressure. No demands. She wanted so much more, and she slid her hands into his hair, pulled him closer. She yearned for *this,* for him.

She lost herself in the sweetness of the kiss, the gentleness of his touch, her heart thundering wildly, her body humming with need.

"Momma! Help me!" Brady's desperate scream cut through the moment, his terror making Eva's knees weak, her body fluid and loose.

Justice barked. One quick sharp burst of sound that seemed to be coming from Brady's room.

"Brady!" Eva tried to run, but Austin pulled her back.

"Stay here!" he shouted as he ran into Brady's room, his heart pounding double-time, his muscles tight with fear.

Brady seemed to be half asleep, sitting in the middle of his bed, his white-blond hair sticking up in every direction.

That's the first thing Austin noticed.

The second thing he noticed was Justice, his paws resting on the window frame, his nose pressed against the glass. Hackles raised, body stiff, he growled long and low, the warning raising the hair on the back of Austin's neck.

"Did you see something, boy?" He touched the dog's head, and Justice dropped down, his body relaxing as if whatever he'd seen was gone. Austin scanned the area beyond the window. Purple dusk had turned to pitch-black night, deep shadows shrouding the yard. No moonlight. Just darkness upon darkness.

"Brady!" Eva skidded to a stop next to the bed, her face pale, her eyes filled with fear. "What's wrong?"

"He was trying to get in the window. I saw him, Momma. He was coming to get me again." Brady threw himself into her arms, and she sat on the edge of the bed with him, her hair just a shade darker than his, her lips still pink from Austin's kiss.

"Who was trying to get you, sweetie?" She smoothed Brady's hair.

"The man with the brown hair."

"Maybe you were dreaming," she said, but her gaze jumped to the window, then settled on Austin. "Do you see anything?"

"No, and neither does Justice," he said, because the bloodhound lay relaxed and at ease near his feet. Someone *had* been there, though. Austin didn't say that. Not in front of Brady. The poor kid was already scared enough.

"See, Brady? Everything is okay. If it wasn't, Justice would be barking and growling."

"But I saw him, Momma. I really did. Justice growled, and I looked, and he was right there," Brady insisted, but he sounded tired, his eyes drifting closed as he leaned against Eva.

"Whatever you saw is gone now. Go to sleep, sweetie." She eased Brady onto his pillow, covered him with a thick, blue blanket, kissed the fading bruise on his forehead and motioned for Austin to follow her into the hall.

His hair was mussed from her hands, his eyes blazing. The feel of his lips was still warm on hers. She wanted to throw herself back in his arms and tell him how scared she was. Wanted to listen as he told her everything would be okay.

She wrapped her arms around her waist instead, glancing into the room. Brady lay still and silent. Probably sound asleep again.

"Justice saw something, didn't he?" she whispered.

"Yeah."

"Could it have been a deer or a mountain lion? Maybe a bear?" That's what she wanted it to be. Any one of those things would be better than the alternative.

"Justice doesn't growl or bark at animals. I'm going to take him out back. I'll knock when we're finished."

"Austin..." She didn't know what she wanted to say, her thoughts lost in the swirl of dread that filled her mind and drove everything else away.

"It's going to be okay, Eva." He cupped her shoulders, his palms warm through her T-shirt, his gaze steady. She'd spent her life wondering what it would be like to have someone she could really depend on. As she looked into Austin's eyes, she thought she finally knew.

"I hope you're right."

Austin did, too. He squeezed Eva's hand, dropped a kiss on her forehead. "I'll be back as soon as I can."

Austin hooked Justice to his lead and led him

out the back door, using his flashlight to illuminate the dark edges of the yard.

Justice snuffled the ground as they moved toward Brady's window. The bloodhound paused there, huffing deeply as he nosed the grass.

"What do you smell, boy?" Austin crouched near the house, studying the packed earth beneath the window. No footprints visible, but that didn't mean no one had been there.

"Something going on out here? I saw a light and thought I'd better check things out." The patrol officer who'd been sitting guard out front walked around the corner of the house. Older than Austin by a couple of decades, he had the confident walk and the straightforward air of someone who knew his job and did it well.

"Brady thought he saw someone looking in the window at him."

"If he did, the person didn't walk around from the front of the house."

"It would have been easy enough for someone to cut through the back neighbor's property without being seen. It's black as pitch out here," Austin replied, and the patrol officer nodded.

"True. Did your dog alert?"

"He saw something."

"How about I dust for prints? See if we come up with anything on the sill?"

"Sounds good. I'll see if Justice can pick up a

scent and track it. I'll radio in if we find anything. Seek," he commanded.

Responding immediately, Justice inhaled deeply, his body trembling with excitement as he raced through the neighbor's backyard and onto the street beyond it.

SIXTEEN

Midnight and still no sign of Austin.

Exhausted, Eva paced the living room for another hour and finally gave up her vigil. She changed into flannel pajamas and climbed into bed next to Brady. He seemed to be sleeping nightmare free, his body limp and his breathing deep. Good. After a couple of restless nights, he needed his sleep.

Eva did, too, but she couldn't make herself relax enough to drift off. Every creak of old wood, every groan of wind in the eaves reminded her that someone might have been stalking the house just a few hours ago.

Stalking Brady.

Please, God, let the police find the second kidnapper soon. Please keep Brady safe until they do, she prayed silently.

Brady whimpered in his sleep, and she smoothed his hair and kissed his forehead, finally giving up on the idea of rest. She went to her room and dug through her dresser drawer. Her mother's Bible was there. Unlike the hardcover Bible Eva usually read from, her mother's was soft, worn leather and still held just a hint of the cheap perfume that Tonya had worn every day of her life for as long as Eva could remember.

Eva carried it into the living room and flicked on the lamp, the soft, golden glow chasing away the darkness and some of her fears. She pulled back the curtain, making sure the patrol car was sitting at the curb.

Still there.

And still no sign of Austin.

He'd said that he'd stop back in when he was finished his search, so where was he?

Had he been attacked? Overcome? Injured?

She tried to push away the thoughts. It didn't do any good to speculate. But she couldn't seem to help herself. She kept imagining his body lying bleeding and broken somewhere. Imagined him in desperate need of help with no one to turn to.

"Stop it!" she hissed, settling on the couch and curling up under the afghan Mrs. Daphne had given her for Christmas. She felt cold to the bone, her body aching with it, her teeth chattering. If she hadn't been completely terrified by the thought, she'd have walked into the backyard and grabbed a couple of pieces of firewood from the pile, started a fire in the fireplace.

She *was* terrified, though, so she stayed put, pulling the afghan closer and letting the Bible fall open, knowing exactly which passage it would fall to. Isaiah 40:31.

But those who hope in the Lord will renew their strength. They will soar on wings like eagles; they will run and not grow weary, they will walk and not become faint.

The words were underlined and highlighted, the page stained with years' worth of tears that had flowed because Tonya had married a criminal, a rake, a liar, a thug. Tears that had fallen because she'd felt trapped by her commitment and the love that had made her weak.

So many tears.

Eva's first memory was of her mother crying. She'd been five or six and peeking out of her room after Ernie stormed from the trailer. She could still remember the knot in her stomach as she'd watched her mother pick up the shattered plates and the old clock that Ernie had destroyed. Tonya had been young. Maybe twenty-four, but she'd moved like an old woman, bending slowly as if every bone hurt. When she was done, she'd pulled the Bible from its hiding place under the couch cushions and lowered herself into the old rocking chair, tears pouring down her face, her lips moving as she read words that should have comforted her.

Eva didn't want to be that woman, rocking to the rhythm of her sorrow. She didn't want to be so in love with someone that she lost every bit of who she was.

She wanted a love that built rather than tore down. A relationship that made her better rather than worse.

She wanted the dream she'd had when she was a kid. The happy home and the loving husband.

Someone knocked on the door, the soft sound pulling Eva from the past. Austin. She didn't have to look to know it was him. She swiped her hand over the Bible's wrinkled page, trying to wipe away the memory of her mother's tears, her hand shaking, her heart beating hard and heavy as she walked to the door.

She felt sick with the memories of her mother, tired in a way that she hadn't been since she'd found Tonya lying in a pool of her own blood, her hand reaching for her husband's. Even in death. Even after she'd given the last bit of what she had for him.

Eva opened the door, crisp winter air gusting in and cooling her heated cheeks, her heart leaping as she looked into Austin's eyes.

If anyone could ever be her happily-ever-after, it was him.

The thought whispered into her heart, lodged there and she couldn't deny it.

"Sorry it's so late. I wouldn't have knocked, but I saw your light go on, and I thought you'd like an update," Austin said quietly as he unhooked Justice's leash and stepped inside.

"I was up waiting for you, so you don't have to apologize." Her voice sounded gravelly and thick with the tears that she didn't want to shed.

Tears for her mother.

For herself.

Tears for the things that could have been if Tonya had only been strong enough.

"Are you okay?" he asked gently, pulling her into his arms and pressing her head to his chest.

She knew she should back away, deny herself the comfort that he offered, but she wanted to stand there with him almost as badly as she wanted to take her next breath. Her hands slid beneath his coat, her heart thudding painfully, her breath coming in a quick dry sob.

"Eva?" He eased back, looked into her face. "What is it, honey?"

"Why can't you be a horrible person, Austin? Why can't you be untrustworthy and mean? If you hated children and kicked puppies and chewed tobacco, it would be so much easier to walk away from you."

"Who says you have to walk away?" He smiled

a little, running a knuckle down her cheek, sliding it over her bottom lip.

"Me."

"Why?"

"Because I'm a coward."

"You aren't even close to being that." He pressed a gentle kiss to the palm of her hand, closed her fingers over it, and her entire body shuddered with longing.

"You're wrong. I'm the biggest coward in the world." She dropped onto the couch, pulled the afghan close. It wasn't nearly as warm as Austin. "Did you and Justice find anyone?"

"We tracked a scent trail for a few miles, but lost it close to downtown."

"So someone really was looking in Brady's window?" She hadn't wanted to believe it, but she couldn't say she was surprised.

"Yes, and there's more. We pulled a print from the windowsill. There was a match for it in our database. That's why I was gone for so long."

"You have a name?"

"Don Frist. He has a rap sheet a mile long. Mostly petty crime, but he was in jail last year on drug-possession charges. I pulled his mug shot. He's our second kidnapper."

"You're sure?" She grabbed his hand, didn't even realize she was holding on to him until his thumb ran across her wrist, the sweeping caress sending heat through her blood.

"Positive. He's the guy I saw in the Lost Woods. We have a warrant out for his arrest. All we have to do is find him."

"What if he comes back before you do?" The thought of him skulking around the house, searching for a way inside, made her stomach churn.

"We've upped police presence in the neighborhood and put a patrol car on the street behind yours. That will make it more difficult for him to access your yard through the neighbor's."

"Difficult, but not impossible."

"No." He paused, ran a hand down his jaw. "Eva, there's something else."

"Go ahead."

"Frist's fingerprints matched some that were pulled from your parents' home after their murders."

"Are you saying that he killed my parents and now he's after my son?" She stood so quickly, she felt dizzy, stars dancing in front of her eyes, darkness sweeping in so unexpectedly that she would have fallen if Austin hadn't grabbed her waist and held her steady.

"Sit back down, Eva, before you pass out."

"I'm not going to pass out." But she sat, anyway. Just in case. "Now, will you please tell me what's going on? Did Frist murder my parents?"

"Aside from the fingerprints, there was no evidence to link him to the crime. He was questioned after his prints were found, and he had an airtight alibi."

"What alibi? A friend vouching for him? A glimpse of him at a bar somewhere?" She sounded bitter and angry. She *felt* bitter and angry. Two years she'd been waiting for a suspect to be named and someone to be arrested, and the police had had Frist's fingerprints all along.

"He was at a wedding in Maine, and he had photos and plane tickets to prove it. He said that his fingerprints were at the crime scene because he was a friend of your father's."

"My father didn't have any friends." He'd had people who he used and people who used him, but no friends.

"The investigating officer thought there might be a criminal connection between the two of them, but that didn't mean that Frist was the murderer."

"It didn't mean he was innocent, either."

"No, but there were other fingerprints at the scene. A couple of sets that were identified. A couple that weren't."

"Why is this the first that I'm hearing of it?" she asked sharply.

"I can't answer that, Eva. I wasn't the investigating officer. If I had been, I'd like to think that I would have been a lot more forthcoming with you."

Her eyes bore into his. "You'd like to *think* it?"

"It would be easy for me to say that I would have been, but sometimes information is kept from the family of the victims out of compassion or concern."

"Right." She walked across the room, tried to wrap her mind around everything he'd told her. "You don't have any proof that Frist murdered my parents, but you do have proof that he was at my house and that he kidnapped Brady. He'll at least pay for that."

"Right, and we're looking for more. We're waiting for a judge to issue a search warrant. Once he does, we'll go into Frist's house and see what we can find."

"In the meantime, Brady is still in danger."

"And will be until we can bring Frist in. I think you need to consider bringing in a tutor while all this is going on. Having him at home rather than school will make it easier for us to protect him."

"A tutor for how long?" she asked.

"For as long as it takes to find Frist."

"That could be months, Austin, and I can't take any more time off work. Arianna has already made it clear that I'd better show up on Wednesday. If I don't, I'll lose pay, and I can't afford that."

"Don't worry. Everything is taken care of," he told her.

"What do you mean?"

"Slade and I agreed that Mrs. Daphne couldn't be Brady's babysitter while you work. We'll have a police officer take over until all this blows over."

"Blows over? You make it sound like a thunderstorm." She sighed, and he smiled, lifting the Bible from beside her and letting it fall open in his hands.

If Tonya had met him, she'd have thought he was exactly the kind of man Eva deserved.

The thought made her eyes burn and her chest tight.

"Yours?" he asked, and she knew he was looking at the tearstains, the underlined words, the pain.

"It was my mother's."

"What was she like?"

What *had* Tonya been like?

When Eva thought of her, all she saw were tears.

"Sad."

"Because she couldn't escape her marriage?"

"She could have left Ernie if she wanted to. She had a degree in elementary education. I found that out after she died. She had plenty of qualifications and the intelligence to make a life for herself and for me. She chose not to."

"Because she loved your father?" he asked.

"Yes, but Ernie didn't love her. He didn't have it in him to love anyone. If he had, maybe things would have turned out differently."

"Eva..." He touched her arm, and she felt a moment of yearning so deep that it shook her to the core.

She didn't want to need him.

Didn't want to need anyone, but being with Austin made her forget all the reasons why. "It's late, Austin. You'd better go."

He didn't argue. Just set the Bible back into place, smoothing a hand over the worn cover like a final benediction before he walked to the door.

"I'll call you as soon as I hear anything about Frist."

"Thanks." She put her hand on the door handle, but he pulled it away, wove his fingers through hers so that their palms were pressed together.

"Just one more thing before I go."

"What?"

"This." His lips grazed hers, the touch so light and unexpected that she didn't feel it until it was over. Didn't acknowledge it until he was gone, the door between them, the thundering pulse of her blood sloshing in her ears.

She touched her lips, felt the warmth that lingered there.

A kiss that took nothing and gave everything,

that's what he'd offered, and she'd taken it because she hadn't had the strength to turn away.

She sighed and turned off the light, grabbing her mother's Bible as she walked to Brady's room.

SEVENTEEN

Spending five days housebound with an energetic seven-year-old was enough to drive any mother to the brink of insanity, Eva thought as she poured cereal into Brady's bowl and tried to explain why he still wasn't ready to go back to school.

At least it was Wednesday. Her first day back at work.

She was happy to be getting out of the house. Not so happy to be leaving Brady at home. Even if she was leaving him with a police officer.

"But, I *am* ready to go back to school, Momma. I caught up on all the work I missed and everything," Brady told her as he spooned up a bite of cereal.

"I know you feel ready, Brady, but you can't go back until the police find the man who took you. Until then, they want you to stay home where they can keep their eyes on you."

"But *you're* going to work. Why can't I go to school?"

"I *have* to work or we won't have money to pay the bills. You can miss a couple more days of school. You're smart enough to get caught up."

"But can't I come with you, Momma? We haven't gone anywhere in days and days."

"Not today, but as soon as Austin says it's safe, I'll take you to Arianna's for pancakes."

"Okay." He sighed and poked at the cereal. He'd slept restlessly the past few nights, still plagued by the nightmares he'd been having since the kidnapping. But his eyes weren't as deeply shadowed, his cheeks not as gaunt.

"Maybe after we have pancakes, we can go to the park. You can invite a few of your friends over and we'll all go together."

"That would be fun, I guess."

"You guess? You've been asking me to take you to the park for months." She'd been too busy working and going to school and doing all the things that she'd thought would make their lives better to bring him before. Now she realized how quickly everything she'd been working for could disappear, and she wanted to make sure that she spent time having fun with Brady while she could.

"I don't know if I want to go to the park."

"We can go somewhere else, then." She ruffled Brady's soft hair, knowing that he was as scared to go out as he was anxious to leave. She felt the same, torn between the need to get back to her life and her fear that something worse would happen to Brady once they ventured out again.

"You know what I really want to do, Momma?" He shoved the nearly full cereal bowl away.

"What?"

"I want to go for a walk with Austin and Justice. If we went for a walk with them, we'd be safe."

"That sounds nice."

Really nice.

So nice that she was tempted to call him up and ask him if he wanted to do it right at that very moment.

She pressed her fingers to her lips, sure she could still feel the heat of his kiss, realized what she was doing and let her hand fall away.

So silly to be pinning dreams on him.

Especially when he hadn't been back to visit since Don Frist had been fingered as the second kidnapper. He'd called, though. Quite a few times, just checking in and giving updates. Talking about work and asking her about school and about Brady.

Normal mundane conversations that had made her heart soar and her pulse sing.

"Will you call and ask if he'll come take me for a walk, Momma?"

"You know he's busy, Brady. He's trying to catch your kidnapper."

"Why is everyone busy but me?" he whined.

"You'll be busy soon enough. Your tutor is coming today, remember?"

"I don't want a stinky old tutor—"

"Brady Billows! That is an awful thing to say when the school has worked so hard to find someone to teach you at home."

"Sorry, Momma."

"Just make sure you don't call her stinky and old again," she chided, "Especially not when she's here. If you do, that puppy we've been talking about won't happen for a long time."

"I won't say it to her or anyone else. Promise."

"Good." She kissed his head, shoved his bowl back in front of him. "Eat."

"Mrs. Daphne always makes me waffles and eggs when I don't have school."

She sighed. "I'm not Mrs. Daphne."

"Is she coming over today?"

"No, but there *will* be someone else with you besides the tutor."

"Who? A police officer?"

"I think so."

"Will he have a gun?"

"I don't know, Brady. How about we just wait and see?"

"I hope that he *does* have a gun, but what I really want is for him to have a dog like Justice. Then I'll have someone to play with all day."

"That would be fun." Eva poured coffee into her mug, searched the refrigerator for cream that she knew wasn't there. No milk, either. She'd used the last on Brady's cereal.

"I could even take the dog outside—"

"No."

"Just in the backyard."

"Brady, I mean it. If you go outside, I'm going to have to take all your Legos away for at least a week."

"Okay. I won't go outside. But I *can* play with the dog, right? I can take it into my room?"

"We don't even know if there's going to be a dog, but if there is, and the officer says it's safe, you can play with it." Eva went into the bathroom to run a brush through her hair, scowling at the reflection in the mirror. She wasn't one to spend much time worrying about her appearance, but there were days when she'd love to get her hair done, maybe paint her nails, put on a little makeup. Today was one of them. Dark circles under her eyes, pallid complexion, she looked like a before ad for a cosmetic procedure.

She pulled her hair into a high ponytail. Comfy shoes for all-day walking, a slight hint of blush and gloss and she was ready. She just needed Brady's bodyguar—*babysitter* to arrive.

"Momma! Someone is ringing the doorbell!"

Brady hollered, and she grabbed her purse, rushed to the door and opened it.

"Next time, you might want to ask who it is first," Austin said as he and Justice walked in. Dark windblown hair, his jaw stubbled by several days' growth, he looked good. Really good.

"I was just on my way out. I'm opening the diner this morning," she said.

"That's why I'm here."

"You're not..."

"What?" His smile said it all. *He was.*

"Austin, you said a police guard. You didn't say it was going to be you."

"I don't trust anyone else with Brady's life," he said, and her heart melted, every bit of her resistance melting with it.

"You're staying with me, Austin?" Brady said, and he sounded like he'd just won the lottery.

"I sure am. Want to go get those blocks you like to play with? I'm thinking we should build something giant today."

"Really? Mrs. Daphne never plays with me!" Brady ran to Eva and gave her a kiss goodbye before disappearing down the hall.

"You've made his day," Eva said, still not sure how she felt about it.

"And you've made mine. You look beautiful this morning." He tugged her close, gave her an easy hug that should have been friendly and felt like so much more.

"I'm a mess. Between a sleepless night and not much time to get ready, I—"

"You're beautiful. End of story."

"Austin—"

"Better get going, or you're going to be late. Based on what I saw when Arianna visited you at the hospital, I'd say that won't be a good thing."

Eva nodded, but she couldn't bring herself to walk out the door.

"You know I'm going to take good care of him, right?" Austin framed her face with his hands, smiled into her eyes, and every cell in her body strained toward him.

"I know."

"Then why are you hesitating?"

"He's my son. He's everything to me."

"I know, and I'll protect him with my life if I have to. Now go to work, before I do something that I won't regret but that you might." His gaze dropped to her lips.

Her cheeks heated, her pulse raced, and she seriously considered throwing herself right into his arms.

She left instead.

He closed the door, and she heard the bolt slide home.

Locked out of her house.

Well, not quite. She had the keys.

She could go back inside if she wanted to, but Austin was right. She had to get to work. Arianna expected her to be there to open the restaurant, and if she was late, there'd be trouble.

She didn't need that any more than she needed the mess she'd found herself.

Austin at her house, protecting her son while she went to work?

It smacked of domesticity, made her feel soft and vulnerable, but not nearly as scared as she thought she should be.

That was probably a bad thing.

She glanced at the house as she pulled out of the driveway, imagining Austin and Brady side by side on the floor, building a doghouse or a police car or a trap for the bad guys Brady kept dreaming about.

She wanted so badly to go back.

Not because she didn't trust Austin. Not even because she was worried about how much of a fixture he was becoming in her life.

She wanted to go back so that she could watch them together, be part of the laughter and fun. Be…

What?

A family?

Such a strange thing to think, but she couldn't seem to stop herself. When Austin was around, she felt lighter, the weight of some of her responsibilities shifted to his broad and steady shoulders.

That should scare her.

It really should.

So why was she smiling?

Humming along with the radio?

Acting for all the world like a woman who was falling in love?

Love?

She didn't believe in it. Not the kind that lasted, anyway. Not for her.

But just like the happily-ever-after she'd given up believing in, if love were ever going to happen for her, it would happen with Austin.

She frowned, shoving the thought away.

Brady was happy and well protected when he was with Austin. She believed that, and for now, that was all that really mattered.

EIGHTEEN

Babysitting was a piece of cake compared to chasing down clues and following up on leads. Austin scowled at his computer screen. Eight hours at Eva's place, and seven at the office, and he still had nothing to show for his day.

Unless he counted the block jail that he'd built with Brady.

He took a sip of lukewarm coffee.

Five days after Brady's kidnapper had been identified, and Frist was still free. Too bad, because Austin would have loved to have personally locked the guy up and thrown away the key.

He tapped his pen against his desk, eyeing the evidence list and the case file. With a twenty-five-thousand-dollar reward on the line, it seemed like someone should have come forward with information by now, but the silence was deafening and the case seemed to be grinding to a slow halt. Even Keevers hadn't followed up on his promise of big information.

Justice whined from his place beneath the desk, and Austin patted the bloodhound's knotty head. "Sorry, boy, this is about as exciting as it's going to get tonight."

"Are you still here, Austin? It's a little late, isn't it?" Slade walked toward him, his steps brisk. Past midnight and they were both at the office. Obviously, neither of them were happy with the progress that was being made on the case.

"I spent most of the day at the Billowses, and I wanted to do a little work here before I went home. See if I could make heads or tails of the information we've gathered."

"And?" Slade pulled a chair over.

"Until we find Frist, we're at a standstill."

"At least he hasn't gone after Brady again."

"*Yet.* He's gone to ground, but that doesn't mean he's out of the picture for good."

"Any contact with Keevers?"

"He hasn't called. Parker said that he's been quiet on the street, too."

"Scared?" Slade asked, and Austin shrugged.

"Could be. Or maybe he's just hoping that if he holds out a little, we'll be desperate enough to go higher on the price."

"I cleared up to fifteen thousand. Any more than that, and we're going to have to pass." Slade snagged Frist's mug shot from Austin's desk. "Have we posted this on our website?"

"Yes."

"And at the post office?"

"Yes. He's been all over the news, too. So has the information about the reward Frears is offering. I'm surprised no one has stepped forward yet."

"You and me both. With that much money on the line, it seems like we should have dozens of rats crawling out of their nests to feed."

"You know why people get quiet, Austin?" the captain set the photo down again. "Fear. And if people around here are afraid, they must have a reason."

"The Boss?"

"That's what I'm thinking. I want to know who he is. I want to know what he's doing in our town. How long he's been here. What crimes he's responsible for."

"Who works for him?" Austin offered.

"That, too. Dante called me this afternoon."

"Yeah?"

"He wanted to check on Caleb, and he wanted to know if we've had anyone come forward with information." McNeal scrubbed a hand across his face. "I hated to tell him that we haven't."

"It could still happen, Slade. We're early in the game."

"We're nearly a week into the game, Austin.

Rio has been missing that whole time. I'm afraid if we don't find him soon, we never will."

"We're going to find him. I won't give up until we do."

"I'm glad to hear that, but you know the statistics. A case not solved within the first forty-eight hours is less likely to ever be solved. The longer the case remains open, the less chance of it being resolved."

"That doesn't mean—" His cell phone rang, and he grabbed it, motioning for Slade to give him a second while he answered. A few minutes past midnight was an odd time for anyone to be calling, and his heart raced with the possibilities.

"Austin Black."

"Hey, Detective, long time, no talk." Pauly's smooth voice oozed through the receiver, and Austin smiled, mouthing the name to his captain.

"Maybe a little too long. I thought you were interested in some cash, but the offer might be off the table now," he responded.

"Now, wait just a minute, Detective. You take the offer off the table, and you may never find that missing dog."

"What are you talking about, Pauly?" Austin straightened in his chair, motioned for Slade to lean in close to the phone.

"I've heard some whispers about your captain's

missing partner, and I thought that maybe you could sweeten the pot to get access to them."

"How sweet do you want it?"

"Just throw in a couple thousand more. Let's make it an even twelve, and I'll tell you everything I know."

"Twelve thousand is a lot of money, Pauly."

"What I know is worth every penny of it."

"We'll see."

"So, it's a deal?" Keevers pressed.

Slade nodded.

"It's a deal."

"Just so we're clear, if the information I give you leads to the mutt, I want the twenty-five-thousand-dollar reward."

"If it helps us find Rio, you'll get the twenty-five thousand, too."

"That's what I wanted to hear. You have that twelve for me?"

"I can have the cash tomorrow." He glanced at Slade who nodded again.

"Good. Meet me at the same place as last time at two in the morning. Don't bring anyone with you, and don't tell anyone but your boss that we're meeting. Not anyone, Black. Otherwise, I might have to leave town, and we'll both be left with nothing."

Keevers disconnected, his words ringing in Austin's ears. He'd sounded scared, and that wasn't like Pauly. As much as he played both sides of the fence, Keevers had never seemed overly concerned about getting caught. Now he was issuing warnings, trying to protect himself.

"That was…interesting," Slade said.

"He sounded nervous."

"I thought the same. Let's hope the information he's offering is as worth it as he's claiming."

"He's never failed us before."

"I know. And I've got to admit that this is getting my blood flowing. Hopefully, it will also breathe some new life into the case. I'll expect to hear from you as soon as your meeting is over."

"You know that you will," he promised.

"Good. Now, how about we both pack up and get out of here?" Slade retreated into his office, and Austin shoved the file into the cabinet, turned off his computer and stretched the kinks out of his back.

"Come on, Justice. Let's go home," he said.

Justice lumbered up from his spot beneath Austin's desk, stretching his long, sturdy body and shaking off the last vestiges of sleep, his jowls slapping back and forth with the force of the motion. Austin scratched the sensitive spot beneath his chin, grinning as the bloodhound nudged his hand for more.

"Sorry, boy. We've got to get going." He attached Justice's leash and led him out into the silent parking lot.

Sagebrush was quiet this time of night. Most reputable establishments closed; most people locked away in their homes. A small city with a rural vibe, it wasn't the kind of place where people partied until all hours of the night. Sure, there were dives and bars where those who wanted to could lose themselves until the sun came up, but those places were few and far between.

That was one of the things Austin loved about this town.

He crated Justice and started the SUV, pulling out onto the deserted road and driving toward home. He hadn't been there since morning when he'd left to go sit with Brady. He'd stayed at the Billows's place listening to Brady's home tutor go over addition with carrying and how to write a friendly letter until Eva arrived home at five. She'd been harried and tired, thanking him absently as he'd rushed out the door. They could have been an old married couple, moving in synch, plugged into each other's lives but somehow distant.

Could have been, except that they weren't married.

Weren't even a couple.

Not in the truest sense of the word.

There was something there, though, their relationship both exciting and fresh and easy and familiar. He'd never experienced that with a woman before, and the power of it had him thinking about Eva way more than he probably should be.

He pulled up in front of his house, the windows dark and uninviting. He should have remembered to leave a light or two on. Not because he feared the dark, but because it made coming home seem so much less lonely.

"Come on, boy. I think lack of sleep is starting to get to me." He let Justice out of the crate and walked to the front door. A box sat on the stoop. Cardboard. Maybe two by three feet and a half foot tall. He hadn't ordered anything, and the box didn't look sealed or sent. No address label. No tape. Nothing.

The hair on his nape stood on end, and he tugged Justice back as the bloodhound tried to nose the box. "Stay!"

The dog subsided, his nose lifted into the air, his body straining forward as if he were desperate to get to the box. Justice wasn't trained in explosive detection but he had a great nose, and whatever was in the box was exciting him.

"Stay!" Austin ordered again, then moved toward the box cautiously. He had no reason to believe he'd be the target of an attack, but better to be safe than dead.

A white envelope rested between the box and

the door, and Austin opened it carefully, letting a slip of paper fall into his hand.

Someone had scribbled across the front:

You were probably too busy to eat dinner. I thought I'd better feed you so you're not stuck with overcooked pasta again. E.

Surprised, he opened the box flaps and pulled out two large plastic containers. He wasn't sure what was in them, but whatever it was smelled good. His stomach rumbled, and Justice whined. Obviously, he was hungry, too.

"Come on. I think it's time for both of us to eat." He carried the box into the house and set it down on the table, fed Justice and let him out in the backyard.

He knew what he shouldn't do. Call Eva and thank her. Especially not at this time of night. He glanced at the clock. This time of *morning.*

He was tempted, though.

Too tempted.

His cell phone rang as he opened up the first container.

"Black, here," he said as he poured thick stew into a bowl and shoved it into the microwave.

"Did you get the food, or did the coyotes drag it away before you got home?"

His heart pounded at the sound of her voice. "I just got it and was thinking about calling you. I thought it might be too late."

"I thought the same thing, and then I started worrying that maybe something had happened to you, and that's why you hadn't..."

"Called to thank you for the food?"

"Yes, but I didn't mean for it to sound like I *expected* you to thank me. It's just... Okay. Maybe I did mean it to sound that way. What I mean is, you're always so polite, and I couldn't imagine that you'd... Never mind." She sighed, but there was a smile in her voice, and he imagined her pale cheeks flushed with embarrassment, her eyes glinting with humor.

"I'm glad you called, and you know it's never too late, right? I'd be happy to answer the phone any time of day if you were on the line."

"Keep sweet-talking me, Austin, and I might have to make pie the next time I bring you dinner."

"What kind?"

"Apple?"

"My favorite." He pulled the stew from the microwave, set it on the table, wishing he were at Eva's house, sitting in her tiny kitchen, looking in her eyes rather than talking to her on the phone. "The stew looks great. When did you bring it over?"

"I asked Mrs. Daphne to drop it off. Now, of course, she thinks we'll be married by fall." The phone clicked, the soft sound repeating twice.

"Is someone trying to call you?" he asked.

"Yes."

"I can let you go—"

"No!" she nearly shouted, and Austin frowned, his hand tightening on the phone.

"What's going on, Eva?"

"I don't know. Probably nothing. It's just, we've been getting phone calls all afternoon. Whoever it is hangs up as soon as anyone answers. It's silly, I know…but it's bothering me."

"Aside from the call you just received, when did you get the last one?"

"Just before I called you."

"And how many calls do you think you've gotten altogether?" he demanded.

"At least one every hour since I got home."

"And you're just now letting me know?" Austin dropped his empty bowl into the sink and paced to the window. Bright moonlight poured onto the yard, painting it in shades of gold and gray. A beautiful winter landscape, but that didn't mean that danger wasn't lurking somewhere in it.

"It seemed like a silly thing to bother you about."

"How about from now on, you let me decide whether or not something is too silly to bother me with?"

"That would kind of defeat the whole purpose of me vetting things so that you can rest."

"I don't need rest, Eva. I need to make sure you and Brady are okay. I'll be there in ten minutes."

"You can't—"

He hung up.

No amount of arguing on her part was going to keep him from driving to her place. Hopefully, once he got there, they'd figure out that there was nothing more to the calls than a wrong number or a persistent solicitor. Somehow, though, he didn't think that was going to be the case.

NINETEEN

She probably shouldn't have called Austin.

She *definitely* shouldn't have called him.

But Eva had been nearly asleep when the phone rang for what seemed like the hundredth time. She'd been drifting into a nightmare where Brady was missing again, and she'd grabbed the phone, confused, still riding the waves of fear. She'd pressed the receiver to her ear, heard nothing but the soft sound of empty air. There'd been something awful in that emptiness, as if the person were right outside the window, watching as she lay in bed.

The thought had been horrifying, and she'd found herself reaching for her cell phone and dialing Austin's number. She hadn't wanted him to come over. She'd just wanted to hear his voice, ask if he'd gotten the food that Mrs. Daphne had dropped off, pretend that her life was normal and easy and that Austin would always be a part of it.

"And so what if he isn't? You'll go on, and you'll

be fine," she whispered as she drew back the living-room curtain and looked outside. Moonlight drenched the street in gold, but clouds moved across the horizon. Rain coming, and she could almost feel its energy in the air.

Or maybe that was her own energy.

Restless.

Anxious.

Scared.

The police car sat where it had been all day, the officer offering a quick wave as he caught sight of Eva. She could have flagged him down, had him come in and check things out.

She hadn't.

She knew what that said about her. Knew what it meant.

She couldn't make herself care, though.

Maybe she wouldn't have Austin in her life forever, but having him there now was wonderful.

Lights flashed behind the curtains, and she knew he'd arrived. She didn't wait for him to ring the doorbell or to knock, just opened the door and stepped out onto the porch, standing in the dark while he got out of his car. He ran up the porch stairs, and it felt as though he was coming home.

Her throat clogged, her eyes burned, and she let him pull her into his arms, let her head rest on his chest. Felt his heartbeat beneath her ear.

Felt as if she was exactly where she was supposed to be.

"I'm really sorry, Austin. I shouldn't have called," she said, looking up into his face.

"Of course you should have. Let's go inside and see if we can figure things out." He took her arm, his hand warm against her cool skin, his fingers sliding along her elbow and leaving a trail of fire in their wake. She took a deep breath, trying to clear her mind, but all she managed to do was fill it up with more of Austin. His darkly masculine scent, the clean crisp fragrance of soap and winter air.

He went to the phone, lifting it and scrolling through the last few calls. "An unlisted number, but we should be able to find out where it came from. Did you let the answering machine pick up at all?"

"Once I realized that someone was calling and hanging up, I let it pick up every time except the last." She sat on the couch, her muscles aching from a long work shift and too many hours hunched over schoolbooks.

"Mind if I listen?"

"Knock yourself out, but he didn't leave a message."

Austin pressed play, cocking his head to the side as he listened to empty air. Finally, the last message ended. "He's persistent. I'll give him that."

"Maybe it's a solicitor," she suggested.

"Calling so frequently? I don't think so."

"I'd say a bill collector, but the only debt I have is my house mortgage, and I always pay that on time."

"You're grasping at straws, hoping this isn't connected to Brady's kidnapping." It wasn't a question, but she answered, anyway.

"I'm not grasping. I'm just trying to find a reasonable explanation."

"The only reasonable explanation I can think of is that someone is trying to get under your skin. Maybe force you into making a move that will get you out from under police protection."

"Well, he's definitely managed to get under my skin, but I'm not going to do anything stupid because of it."

"Glad to hear it." He smiled, and the butterflies in her stomach took flight. Again. "I'm going to call this in. See if we can get a bead on where the phone call is coming from. Maybe our perp has finally made a mistake, and we'll be able to bring him in."

"I'll start some coffee. I don't know about you, but I could use some."

"Decaf?"

"If you want." She walked into the kitchen while he made his phone call, plugging in the coffeepot, but keeping the light off. She didn't want to wake Brady.

"We're set. Hopefully, we'll have the phone traced by first light." Austin walked into the room, his voice as quiet as his footsteps. Of course, he'd be thinking about Brady sleeping just down the hall. That's the way Austin was, always thinking about others, planning around them. It made him difficult to resist.

Maybe even impossible to resist.

Did she even *want* to resist him?

She turned away, focusing her attention on the coffee and the cup she was pouring it into. "Want some milk or cream? Mrs. Daphne ran to the store for me. We were running low on supplies."

"Black is fine." He took the mug and sat at the table, his long legs encased in dark denim, his feet in scuffed cowboy boots. Masculine. Strong. Sitting right there at her kitchen table, and Eva wanted to stand behind him, rub the tension from his shoulders, let her fingers slide through his dark hair.

"Cookies?" Her voice was husky, her hand shaking as she pulled a package from the cupboard.

"I think I'll wait and have more stew when I get home."

"You're still hungry?" she asked, telling herself that she wasn't going to offer to heat something up for him, that she'd already done her part by making double what she normally would for dinner and sending Mrs. Daphne to Austin's house with it.

"No, but the stew was so good, I want more."

"I have plenty in the freezer." She started to open the door, ready to do exactly what she'd said she wouldn't, but he grabbed her hand, tugged her so that she was standing between his legs.

"I'm fine." His hands were on her waist, his eyes dark pools that she couldn't seem to look away from.

Didn't even want to try to look away from.

She touched his hair, her fingers trailing through the silky strands. "I like your hair."

"I like you." He stood, his hands sliding up her back and down again.

"Austin..."

"You look beautiful today. Have I told you that?"

"Yes," she whispered, because she had no breath in her lungs, no thoughts in her head.

"Good, because I think that if I live to be a hundred, I'll never forget how you look right now."

"In a flannel robe with my hair scraped back in a braid? I *want* you to forget it."

"It's not going to happen. You know why?"

"No, but I think you're going to tell me."

He laughed, but his eyes were somber. "You're

the only woman I've ever known who hasn't cared that the only time we can get together is late at night or early in the morning, the only woman who hasn't needed full makeup and nice clothes to feel confident. That makes you exceptionally beautiful to me."

Just centimeters separated them, and she put her hands on his chest, not sure if she wanted to push him away or pull him closer.

"You terrify me, Austin, because when you say things like that, all I can think about is just how long I've been waiting to meet someone like you."

"Good," he murmured, his lips grazing the tender flesh behind her ear.

She melted against him, her hands sinking into his hair as their lips met. Every thought, every fear, every caution flying away. She felt raw and open, vulnerable and tender.

A tear slipped down her cheek. Just one tear, and she couldn't stop the rest from falling. They spilled down her face, soaking into Austin's shirt, her body stiff and aching from the effort to stop them.

"Shhh," he whispered.

"I'm sorry."

"Don't be."

"I *am*. I've ruined a perfectly good moment." She sniffed, stepping away from his arms, lifting her coffee cup and trying to sip the warm brew.

"*Perfectly good?* I was thinking it was a little better than that."

His comment surprised a laugh out of her, and she brushed the last of the tears away. "Don't be so wonderful, okay, Austin? It will only hurt more if you walk away."

"I think I told you that I don't plan to do that."

"Does anyone ever plan to?" She sighed.

"What are you really afraid of, Eva? Because I don't think it's me."

"Rick—"

"Don't." He raised a hand, cutting off the words before she could speak them. "I'm not him. I already told you that. If you still can't accept it, maybe it's best if I walk away now."

She should let him go.

It would be easier on both of them.

A quick break now, before they fell any further.

He took a step, and she touched his shoulder, let her hand fall away as he glared into her face. "What?"

"You want to know the truth? I'm terrified that I'll turn out like my mother, sitting in a rocking chair, crying for a guy who never loved her. I'm afraid that I'll waste my life on someone who wouldn't waste a second on me. I'm afraid that all the things I want are going to tie me to something that isn't good for me, and I'll wind up dead in a pool of my own blood, Brady crying over my body."

"That's a lot of fear for someone who says she has faith." He raked a hand through his hair, took a sip of coffee.

"I do have faith. In God. Not in myself."

"Maybe you need to have it in both. And in me. I'd better go. It's late, and we both have busy days tomorrow." He walked out of the kitchen, left her standing there, the taste of his lips still on hers, the heat of his touch still pulsing wildly through her blood, the sound of his words echoing in the empty place in her heart.

TWENTY

Tall trees loomed black against the night sky, the Lost Woods beckoning as Austin parked his SUV near the west entrance and jumped out. Keevers stood next to a small Jeep, his shoulders tense.

"You're late," he said as Austin approached.

"Getting the kind of money you asked for takes time."

"But you do have it?"

Pauly Keevers wasted no time getting to the point of the clandestine meeting. His eyes gleamed in the darkness, his face taut and tense with nerves or excitement. Austin couldn't decide which the snitch was feeling. He wasn't sure it even mattered. One way or another, he planned to get what he'd come for.

"Only if you have the information we agreed to exchange it for."

"Let me see the cash. *Then* we'll talk."

"You don't hold all the cards here, Pauly, and we're going to do things my way," Austin responded.

"Hey, I'm willing to play it your way. I just want to make sure this is worth my time."

"It is." Austin flipped open the narrow briefcase he and Slade had filled with cash just an hour ago. Twelve thousand dollars was a lot of money to pay for information that might lead nowhere, but it wasn't much at all if it led to Don Frist or Rio.

"Wow-wee, Detective. That sure is a pretty pile of cash. I'm glad you came prepared to deal." Pauly whistled under his breath.

The Lost Woods rustled behind him, dozens of animal eyes staring out from the shadowy underbellies of the trees. Pauly didn't seem to notice. He was too busy eyeing the money in the case. Probably trying to count it.

"I wouldn't be here if I wasn't. Now, how about you give me the information, so that we can make our exchange, and we can both be on our way?" Austin snapped the briefcase closed, and Pauly flinched.

"Okay, but remember, you didn't hear this from me. As a matter of fact, you never even spoke to me."

"Isn't that the way it always works?"

"Yeah, but this time it has to work even better. I don't want anyone knowing. Not cops. Not friends. No one."

"No problem."

"Okay, then. Here's the deal. There's a crime

syndicate working under the radar in Sagebrush. Been there for years, pulling jobs like that big bank heist a few years back. You remember the one? A hundred thousand dollars stolen?"

"I remember." Austin hadn't worked the case, but he'd known about it. A teller had been murdered during the robbery, and the local news had run the story for weeks.

"I don't know much about the syndicate, but the guy who runs it is called The Boss. Rinehart worked for him. So does Frist."

"You know an awful lot about an organization you're not involved in," Austin said as he ran through the details in his mind. So far, everything Keevers said coincided with what they knew.

"I know what I hear, and I've been hearing things for years. I hear about a drug deal and The Boss is mentioned. Bank robberies are mentioned, and The Boss's name is whispered. The guy has been throwing money around and using it to grab more money."

"Be more specific, Pauly. I can't go anywhere with hints and vague references."

"You got a pen?" Pauly didn't wait for Austin to pull out his notebook. He started listing several major crimes that had never been solved. Bank heists, murders, pharmaceutical thefts.

"Are you sure this is all related to The Boss?"

"As sure as I am that you're standing in front of me with a boatload of cash."

"If he's got so much money to throw around, why aren't you working for him?" Austin eyed Pauly, wondering if the information was something fabricated to throw Sagebrush P.D. off Frist's tail.

"No way would I get involved in a scheme with a guy like The Boss. Not even if he paid me a hundred times what you've got in that case."

"I thought you'd do anything for cash."

"Not deal with a guy like him. He has a reputation for making sure people don't talk. The way I hear things, he'd kill his own mother if she got in the way of something he wanted."

"I'm guessing you know a few people who got in his way," Austin prodded.

"Ernie Billows for one," Pauly confirmed with a nod. "Look what happened to him and that pretty wife of his."

"You're saying The Boss killed them?"

"*Had* them killed. I don't think The Boss likes to get his hands dirty."

"Why kill Ernie?"

"Guy was threatening to go to the police with some syndicate names if he didn't get paid more for a job he'd done. The Boss made sure that he didn't get the chance."

"Any idea who the hit man was?"

"I have an idea, but it'll cost you more."

"Then how about you just tell me about Rio. Where is he?"

"That, I can't tell you. I do know this. The Boss hired Frist and Rinehart to take the captain's dog. I heard that straight from the horse's mouth."

"Which horse?"

"Rinehart. A couple hours after the dog was taken, I was behind Arianna's Café finishing up a deal. You know the place?"

"Yeah." Austin didn't ask what kind of deal it was. Knowing Pauly it could have been anything from exchanging information to exchanging drugs for money.

"So, I'm back there and I hear someone coming. Thought it might be one of your guys, so I hid behind the Dumpster. That's when I realize it's Rinehart and Frist. Both are steaming mad and arguing over finishing some job they've been paid to do. Frist says he wants nothing to do with it. He's done. Rinehart says that he'd better not cross The Boss or he'll wake up on the wrong side of eternity. Frist says that he got the dog, and that's all he was paid to do."

"And?"

"That's it. I didn't hear anything else, and I didn't put two and two together until I heard the story about the missing dog and the missing kid. That's when I figured that they must have been talking about nabbing Rio and finishing off the job by getting rid of the boy."

"You should have been a police detective, Pauly."

"Funny. Now, how about my money?"

"Not yet. Why does The Boss want Rio?"

"I hear that he lost something really valuable out here in the wilderness, and the captain's dog is the only one who can find it. Now, how about that cash?"

"One more thing before I hand it over to you, Pauly... Where's Frist?"

"That I can't help you with. He's still in town. I know that, but he's lying low. Don't know if he's more afraid of The Boss or the police. Probably The Boss. If I were him, I would be." He shuffled his feet impatiently. "Now, the money, Detective? We did have a deal, after all."

Austin knew Pauly well enough to know they were finished. He wouldn't get any more information out of the snitch, and that suited Austin just fine. Slade and the rest of the K-9 Unit were back at the station waiting for Austin to return with the information, and he was anxious to bat the stuff around a little. See what they could make of it.

"It's yours." He thrust the briefcase into Pauly's waiting hands.

"And there may be more if you get Rio back, right? You find the dog because of something I told you, I get the 25K reward. That's what you said on the phone, and I'm holding you to it."

"See you, Pauly."

"Now, wait a minute, Detective," Pauly sputtered.

Austin ignored him.

He had bigger fish to fry.

He climbed into his SUV, mulling over Pauly's words.

A crime syndicate made sense and meshed with what the K-9 Unit had already begun to suspect. Like every other city, there'd been crime in Sagebrush over the years. No one had ever connected any of it to an organized effort, though.

But there *was* something bigger going on.

The bank heists alone had netted someone close to a million dollars.

Austin wanted to know who that someone was, and he wanted to see him taken down.

He *would* see him taken down.

Now that they knew what they were dealing with, the Special Operations K-9 Unit would respond the way they always had. They'd come together, work toward the common goal, and eventually, they'd put The Boss behind bars where he belonged.

The first step to doing that was finding Frist.

They had to track him down and keep Brady safe while they were doing it. From the sound of things, The Boss wasn't eager for them to succeed. He'd sent Frist and Rinehart to silence Brady, and that hadn't worked.

Would he come after Brady himself if Frist were taken into custody?

Based on everything Austin knew, he didn't think so. The kingpin of a crime syndicate didn't get where he was by being stupid. Brady was the sole witness to Rio's theft. The only people at the scene had been Rinehart and Frist. Once both men were out of the picture, there would be no need to dispose of the boy, because he wasn't an inherent threat to The Boss.

He was still a threat to Frist, though.

The guy must be in panic mode, trying to find the quickest way out of the trouble he was in.

Austin frowned, glancing at the clock on the dashboard. It was late. Just past two, but he knew Eva would be up studying. He shouldn't call.

But knew he would, anyway.

He waited until he reached the police station, then dialed her number.

She picked up on the first ring.

"Hello?" she said, her voice breathless.

"Did I wake you?"

"No. I was studying."

"I thought you would be," he said softly.

"Just like I thought you'd be the only one who'd call my cell phone at this time of the night."

"You mean aside from your crank caller?"

"I haven't gotten one call from him since yesterday."

"That doesn't surprise me. We were able to track the cell signal to a prepaid phone that someone threw in a trash can downtown."

"Any fingerprints on it?" she asked eagerly.

"You're getting pretty good at this detective stuff, Eva."

"Hardly." She laughed, but he could hear the tension in her voice. "What are you really calling about, Austin?"

"I'm worried about you and Brady."

"Haven't you always been?"

"Yes, but things feel different tonight."

She released a sharp breath. "Because you met with the snitch?"

"Yes."

"I guess you're not going to tell me anything that he said?"

"I can't. Just be careful, okay? Stay inside. Don't make yourself or Brady an easy target."

"I'm going to take that to mean that you're no closer to finding Frist?"

"We're not, but he's not the only one I'm worried about," Austin admitted. "There may be something bigger going on than we first thought, and there may be some very dangerous people who are willing to play for keeps."

"You mean Rinehart and Frist aren't?"

"I mean they weren't the ones calling the shots."

"Be careful, then, Austin. I'd hate for anything to happen to you."

"The feeling is mutual."

"And keep me posted about Frist, okay? Brady is going stir-crazy being locked up inside all the time."

"What about you? Are you going stir-crazy, too?"

"With my crazy schedule? Hardly."

"Too bad," he murmured.

"Why do you say that?"

"I was going to offer to come over after my meeting and take you for a walk in your back-yard."

She snickered softly. "That sounds…danger-ous."

"You and me and a moonlit night? It definitely would be."

"What moon? It's about to rain." She laughed, the sound husky and warm. He felt it to his core, imagined her hair sliding through his fingers, the feel of her lips against his.

Soft.

That's how she'd felt in his arms, and he wanted more of it. More of her.

"If it rains, we'll just sit inside and have some coffee. I can even help you study."

"That sounds even more dangerous."

"Then maybe we'd better wait until the sun comes up," Austin suggested, and Eva wasn't sure if she was more relieved or disappointed.

"Tomorrow, then? I have the day off." And Brady would be awake and a welcome distraction. Definitely a good thing when it came to being around Austin.

"Sure. I'll be there around ten. See you then."

She smiled as she hung up, because that's what Austin did to her. Made her comfortable and happy in a way she hadn't been in a very long time.

She shoved her cell phone into the pocket of her jeans, grabbed the book that she'd been studying and turned off the living-room light. Talking to Austin had been the perfect end to her day, and she was ready for some sleep.

She changed into pajamas and walked into Brady's room, standing over his bed and touching his soft hair as she prayed for him. From the day he was born, all she'd wanted was to give him the life he deserved. It's what she'd been working toward for years. She'd wanted her love for her son to be her focus, wanted him to always feel secure and safe in her heart. She'd worried that bringing a man into her life would change what she'd worked so hard to build.

Truth was, Austin *had* changed things.

He'd made them better, his presence opening the world up for Brady, giving him a taste of what it meant to have an honorable man in his life.

But what if it didn't work out?

What if the things she and Austin felt were fleeting rather than permanent?

Could she risk Brady's heart?

Did she even have a choice anymore?

Brady loved Austin and Justice. Eva saw that every time the two showed up to babysit and every time they left. No matter what happened between her and Austin, that bond had to be maintained.

She sighed, touching Brady's hair one last time before leaving the room.

Maybe this was what faith meant—plunging headfirst into the water without knowing how deep it was, trusting that no matter what, things were going to be okay.

Letting go of the past to grab on to an unknown future.

She'd always thought that she couldn't do any of those things because of Brady. Now she thought that she *must* do those things *because* of him.

She went to the living-room window, pulled back the curtains and stared out into the night, her thoughts spinning so fast that she knew she'd never fall asleep.

Since her parents' murders, she'd had her life planned out. She'd made sure that everything went according to that plan. No veering from the course she'd set. No getting distracted or taking the chance that she'd make a mistake. She'd been sure that was the way God wanted it, had convinced herself of that.

Maybe she'd been wrong.

Maybe all this time, all this fighting to make things be the way she'd thought they should be had gotten in the way of allowing God to make things into what they were meant to be.

Her chest burned with the thought, her mind going back to the kiss she and Austin had shared mere hours ago. The heat of it had lingered long after he'd gone, but it had been the comfort he'd offered when she'd cried that Eva would never forget. The sweetness of his words, the gentleness of his hands, the comfort of his arms. She'd wanted to stay there forever. Such a foolish longing, but it hadn't felt foolish. It had felt like finally coming home.

Rain began to fall, splashing against the window and roof, sliding into puddles on the ground.

She really needed to go to bed. She really did, but she stood for a moment longer, staring out into the night, imagining a future with Austin in it.

Something shifted in the darkness, a shadow moving along the sidewalk, heading toward the police cruiser parked beneath the streetlight.

A dog?

No. A child. Very small. Maybe three or four. Out in the rain. Alone. Shocked, Eva ran to the door, turned off the alarm, was almost down the porch steps when the patrol officer got out of his car.

"Go on back inside," he called. "I'll check things—" He crumbled to the ground, his body a heap of dark cloth and pale skin.

She ran toward him, heard a soft pop, fell back, breath gone. Thoughts gone.

Get up. Get in the house. Get to Brady.

She struggled to her feet, stumbled up the porch stairs. Footsteps pounding behind her. On pavement. On grass.

Go!

She fell into the house, red streaking the white door as she fumbled with the lock. Blood pounding in her ears, sliding down her arm. Head swimming as the lock finally found its home.

Something slammed into the door, the impact reverberating through the wood. Through Eva.

She scrambled back, blood dripping onto hardwood, staining the receiver as she lifted the phone and dialed 911.

TWENTY-ONE

Please, God, let me get there in time. The prayer screamed through Austin's mind, matching the screeching frenzy of sirens as he raced down Oak Street. He had to make it in time. There was no other option. No other acceptable outcome.

Please, God.

He pulled the SUV into Eva's driveway, his blood running cold as he jumped from the vehicle, saw the door hanging open. No alarm. Eva must have turned it off at some point.

Please.

"Austin! Hold up!" Slade shouted, but he didn't wait. Couldn't. Not with Brady and Eva's lives hanging in the balance.

He entered the house silently, easing in through the open door. Darkness. Silence. No sign of a struggle. Nothing but wet footprints tracking across hardwood. Drops of blood on Eva's throw rug. His pulse raced, but he moved slowly, following the sound of rain and wind into the kitchen and the open back door. Something lay in the threshold. Brady's little stuffed dog. Austin left it and walked into the yard. More darkness, rain splattering onto the wet grass, the sound hushed and expectant.

Someone called out, the cry cut off abruptly.

Austin pivoted, running in the direction of the sound. Around the side of the house, skidding to a stop as he caught sight of dark shadows writhing on the ground.

"Freeze!" he shouted, but he didn't pull his firearm. Couldn't risk a shot when he didn't know where one person began and the other ended.

"Austin!" Brady called, and every muscle in Austin's body tensed, every nerve jumping as he turned, saw the little boy running toward him, bare feet splashing in puddles, pajamas clinging to his skinny frame.

"No. Brady, don't!" Eva tried to yell, but the words barely escaped. She clawed at the hands squeezing her throat, stealing her breath. There. Then gone. The scent of alcohol and rage lingering as her attacker pulled out a gun, aimed.

"No!" The words tore from her throat, cold rain falling onto slick grass, sliding down her frozen cheeks. She tried to grab the man's legs, pull him off balance, but her body refused her brain's commands.

A sharp quick report sliced through the darkness, and something warm and heavy landed on her chest and stomach. She wanted to scream, but she had nothing left. Wanted to shove the weight away, but she could only slide deeper into darkness.

"Eva!" Austin's voice carried through the blackness, faint, but so insistent, she couldn't ignore it.

"I'm okay," she mumbled, forcing her eyes open, looking into his face. How had she not realized who he was the first time that she'd seen him? How had she not looked into his face then, and known that she was seeing forever?

She blinked, clearing her eyes and still seeing what he was. What he could be. If she allowed it. She wanted to tell him that, reached out to touch his cheek, but the words didn't come and her hand seemed glued to the muddy ground.

"Brady?" she managed as he lifted her hand, squeezed gently.

"He's safe."

"Where...?"

"With another officer." Austin looked over his shoulder, said something to whoever was behind him. Slade maybe, but Eva couldn't see the details through the thick mist of pain.

"That man...Don Frist—"

"Alive, but he's going to wish he weren't."

"Did—"

"No more talking, Eva." He touched her lips,

his fingers as cold as the pouring rain, but somehow warm, too.

"Ma'am?" An EMT shoved in next to Austin and leaned over Eva, his fingers probing her wrist.

"I'm okay," she said, because it had to be true for Brady's sake.

"You will be." He pressed something to her shoulder and waves of pain rolled over her, chasing away every thought. Darkness again, and then she was moving, floating across golden fields and green grass, blue sky above. No. Lights above. Bright and yellow, Austin's face so close she could feel his breath on her cheek, see flecks of silver in his eyes.

"Hang on, Eva. Brady needs you. *I* need you," he growled, the fear in his voice matching the cold erratic thud of her heart.

I need you, too, she wanted to say, but he was gone before she could, the ambulance sirens screaming as she slipped away again.

Hours later. Days? Eva didn't know, just heard the quiet beep of a machine, smelled the faint metallic scent of dried blood and antiseptic. She tried to sit up, but pain shot through her shoulder and down her arm, blinding her and stealing her breath.

"Brady," she whispered, because he was her first thought.

"He's fine. One of our K-9 officers is with him

in the waiting room." Austin stepped into view, his hair damp, his jaw dark with stubble. He had been her second thought, but not by much.

"How are you feeling?" He brushed hair from her cheek, his palm resting there.

Like she'd been run over by a truck, but she couldn't get the words out. Just covered his hand with hers, pressing his palm more firmly to her cheek. She held on tight. Afraid that if she didn't, she'd float away again.

"That good, huh?" he asked.

"I need to see Brady."

"They won't let him in the ICU."

"I need to see him, anyway, and he needs to see me. He needs to know that I'm okay. Then I need to find someone to take care of him while I'm at the hospital. I need—"

"You were shot and the bullet came within an inch of your heart. What you need is to rest and recuperate. I'll take care of everything else."

"I think you're too good to be true, Austin," she whispered, and he smiled, his eyes soft.

"I'm sure you won't be saying that in another year or two or ten."

"Will you still be around in ten years?"

"Do you want me to be?" His hand slipped from her cheek, skimmed her shoulder, wrist and palm. Pressed close to hers, their fingers linked as if it had always been that way. The two of them fac-

ing the world together, a combined force working to protect Brady and provide the best for him.

Could it really be that easy?

Or would it all fall apart as quickly as it had
happened?

She couldn't know, but she had to try.

"I want you around for as long as you want to
be here."

"Good, because I'm thinking forever sounds
like the right amount of time." His lips brushed
hers, light and gentle as a butterfly's wings, and
her eyes burned with a hundred dead dreams and
a million new ones.

A tear slipped down her cheek, and Austin
brushed it away. "Don't cry, Eva. Everything is
going to be okay."

"I know," she said, but everything she'd ever
wanted was right there beside her, and he was so
steady and wonderful and sure that the tears just
kept coming.

Austin brushed more tears from her cheeks,
looked deep into her eyes. "I'll be right back."

She wanted to tell him not to go, but he was
gone before she could. Out the door and away, the
soft beep of the machine and the quiet hiccup of
her breath the only sounds in the room.

Minutes later he was back, Brady in his arms, a
nurse running behind him. "Detective, you can't
bring him in there—"

"He's her son, and she wants to see him." Austin walked across the room, set Brady down beside the bed. "You'll be careful, right, sport? Your mom is delicate, and we don't want to hurt her."

"I'm not delica—"

"I'll be careful. Hi, Momma. Are you really okay?" Brady's chin quivered, and she knew he was trying hard not to cry. She wanted to pull him onto the bed, hug him close, but pain shot through her chest as she reached for him. She touched his face instead, looked into his blue eyes. She'd almost lost him, but he was there, whole and healthy and safe.

"I am now that I know you are."

"I was so scared, Momma. I thought the bad man was going to kill you." Brady started crying in earnest, and Austin lifted him, patting his back and murmuring something she couldn't hear. Eva watched them together, her eyes growing heavy, the nurse's protests fading. She'd been on her own for so long. There'd been no one else that she trusted as much as she trusted herself to care for Brady. She hadn't thought there would ever be anyone that cared about her son as much as she did. She'd been wrong. Austin could. Did. Would.

The mattress dipped as someone sat on the edge of the bed, and she opened her eyes, looked into Austin's handsome face. Brady lay against his shoulder, eyes closed and body limp as if he'd given everything he had to those last tears and was ready to sleep for hours.

"He needs to be in bed," she said.

"He needs to be with you more."

"The nurse—"

"Agreed that this was best for both of you."

"He's going to get heavy."

"He could never be that." Austin took her hand, squeezing gently. "So how about you do what your son is doing and get some rest? We'll both be here when you wake up."

"I'm glad," she responded, linking her fingers with his again, letting the warmth of his touch, the sweetness of his smile carry her into sleep.

EPILOGUE

Ten days later

"Are they going to be here soon, Momma?"

"*He*. Not they. You know that Austin can't bring Justice into the hospital," Eva responded as she dropped a pile of get-well cards into the flower-print overnight bag that Mrs. Daphne had lent her.

"Let me do that, dear. You're still looking peaked, and I wouldn't want you to wear yourself out before you even get home." Mrs. Daphne took the bag from Eva's hands, her blue-white curls bouncing as she scooped up an oversize flower arrangement and tottered across the room. She placed both on a cart the nurse had wheeled in, setting them next to several other flower arrangements.

"It looks like you have everything," she said. Mrs. Daphne had brought Brady to visit after school and had decided to stay when she'd heard that Eva could finally go home. A good thing, as something as easy as packing an overnight bag seemed too much for Eva's convalescing.

She eased into a chair, wincing as the muscles in her shoulder and chest protested.

"Are you okay, Momma?" Brady hovered next to her, and she tried to smile. He'd been through a lot, and it had taken its toll. Nightmares, anxiety, fear. The counselor had assured Eva that those things would get better in time.

"I'm fine, sweetie. I'll just be happy to get home."

"When did your young man say he would be here?" Mrs. Daphne asked, patting an errant curl into place.

"Around two."

"Well, then, he *will* be here at any moment. While we're waiting, though, I thought I'd get Brady some juice from the cafeteria. He didn't have his snack after school, you know."

"That's fine."

"I'd rather stay with you, Momma," Brady touched her hand, but he didn't cling to it like he had in the first days after she'd been shot.

"If you want to stay, you can. But I'm feeling a little thirsty, too, and I was thinking that if you went, you could get me some juice."

"You're *really* thirsty?"

"I'd *really* like some juice." Because the counselor had said the best way to help Brady was to offer him opportunities to prove to himself that he was safe, that Eva was safe, that everything was the way it had once been.

"Okay. Orange or apple?"

"Orange, of course." She watched as Brady skipped from the room with Mrs. Daphne, then leaned her head back against the wall. Exhausted.

"I think I'm going to have to stick a little closer to your side." Austin's voice cut through the haze of the half sleep Eva had fallen into, and she opened her eyes, smiled.

"Why's that?"

"I leave for a few hours and you wear yourself out." He kissed her gently, the warmth of his lips filled with promise.

"I'm okay. Just resting for the ride home. Brady is a little chatterbox today."

"He's excited that you're finally coming home. Where is the little guy?"

"He went to get juice with Mrs. Daphne. Why?"

"We've had some new developments in the case. I wanted to fill you in while he wasn't around."

"What developments?" She straightened, her heart beating a little faster as she looked into his midnight-blue eyes, saw the concern there.

"Frist is talking."

"That's good, right?"

"Yes, but some of the things he's saying concern you."

"He killed my parents, didn't he?" She'd been hoping for a confession or at least some kind of proof that Frist was responsible. With the future stretching out in front of her, she wanted to close the door completely on the past. Finding her parents' murderer was part of that.

"No, but he says he knows who did. He gave us a name. Charles Ritter."

"I've never heard of him."

"He's a lawyer. A successful one. According to Frist, he is also affiliated with The Boss. Frist says he's middle management. One of three people who may know who The Boss is. According to Frist, Ritter was asked to kill your father as a test of loyalty. Your mother just happened to be—"

"At the wrong place at the wrong time?"

"That's what Frist says. Ritter isn't talking at all. He's lawyered up, but his prints matched some found at your parents' place, and he had a handgun in a safety deposit box. It's the same caliber as the murder weapon."

"So, it's finally over?"

"It is." He brushed strands of hair from her cheek, his fingers gentle and light.

"What about Rio? Has Frist told you where he is?"

"He says he doesn't know. He left him in a crate in an alley downtown. That's the last he saw of him."

"Do you believe him?"

"I don't know. The way I see it, a guy who was desperate enough to use his niece to bait a police officer wouldn't hesitate to tell a few lies to save his own skin."

"Is the little girl finally back with her parents?" Eva could still see the child walking down the sidewalk, tiny and alone, the image etched so deeply in her mind that she didn't think she would ever forget it.

"Not yet. CPS is investigating. Frist's brother knew that Frist was wanted by the police and still let him take his daughter for the night. That's something Child Protective Services is taking seriously."

"Do you think she'll ever be returned to her family?"

"I'm not sure, but I do know one thing."

"What's that?"

"I love you, and I'm glad Frist didn't take you from me."

"I love you, too," she whispered.

"You're not kissing again, are you?" Brady asked as he and Mrs. Daphne walked back into the room.

"I wish," Austin laughed. "You ready to take your mom home, sport?"

"Yep!"

"Then we'd better give her this." He took a

small jeweler's box from his coat pocket, and Eva's heart jumped.

She met his eyes. Saw everything she felt reflected there.

Hope.

Love.

Joy.

"I know what this is!" Brady shouted as he took the box from Austin's hands. His cheeks were flushed, his eyes wide with joy.

"My goodness! What in the world?" Mrs. Daphne edged in close.

"It's the ring Austin bought, Momma. He showed it to me last week, and I've been keeping the secret all this time. And it was really hard." Brady opened the box, took out a beautiful diamond solitaire and handed it to Austin.

"Austin…"

Austin pressed a finger to her lips, cutting off her words. "Let us finish. We worked really hard on the presentation. Ready, sport?"

"Yes."

"Okay. Let's do this thing." Austin took Brady's little hand in his big one, both of them dropping to one knee.

"You are my heart, Eva, and I want to spend the rest of my life with you. Will you marry me?"

"And adopt Justice? Because he wants to be part of the family, too," Brady added, and Eva laughed, joy spilling out in tears that slid down her cheeks. She didn't bother wiping them away as she reached for Austin, allowed him to help her to her feet. She looked into his eyes, felt the truth of his love and said the only thing she could.

"Yes!"

* * * * *

Dear Reader,

Working on a continuity series is always fun. Working on the Texas K-9 Unit continuity was especially exciting. Not only did I get to work with a wonderful group of authors, but I got to incorporate many things that I love into my story—a cute little boy, an adorable and hardworking bloodhound, intrigue, suspense and, of course, romance. What could be better?

Tracking Justice is about more than those things, though. It's about believing that God will work things out even when it is impossible to see how He will do it. It is about trust and faith and moving beyond the past and into a bright and wonderful future. In short, it is about what we all long for and what we all need—hope and second chances.

I hope you enjoy reading *Tracking Justice* as much as I enjoyed writing it! I love to hear from readers. If you have time, drop me a line at shirlee@shirleemccoy.com.

Many blessings!

Shirlee McCoy

Questions for Discussion

1. Eva Billows has had a tough life. What have her experiences taught her?

2. What impact does that have on her relationship with God?

3. Growing up, Eva witnessed her mother's painful marriage. She still tried to find happiness with Brady's father. What decision did she make after that disastrous relationship?

4. Austin Black is dedicated to his job. Finding time for dating is tough. What is it about Eva that makes him question his decision to remain single?

5. How does Austin's faith help him in his decision to pursue Eva?

6. What are Austin's goals and dreams? What does he see in Eva that makes him wonder if she could be part of those things?

7. Eva doesn't believe she can depend on anyone but herself. At what point does she begin to trust Austin?

8. Does her parents' unsolved murder influence her opinion of Austin?

9. Brady is Eva's first priority. What is she afraid might happen if she lets Austin into her life?

10. Do you think her fears are well-founded? Why or why not?

11. Falling in love with Brady's father was a mistake that Eva regrets. Do you think she has forgiven herself for it? Explain.

12. Is Eva able to believe that God has forgiven her?

13. It is clear from scripture that when we repent, God forgives and forgets our transgressions. Why do you think it is difficult for us to do the same?

14. Eva wants to trust God completely. What stands in the way of her doing that?

15. Who do you think took Rio?

LARGER-PRINT BOOKS!

GET 2 FREE LARGER-PRINT NOVELS PLUS 2 FREE MYSTERY GIFTS

Love Inspired®
SUSPENSE
RIVETING INSPIRATIONAL ROMANCE

Larger-print novels are now available...

LISLPDIR13

Love Inspired®

HEARTWARMING INSPIRATIONAL ROMANCE

Contemporary,
inspirational romances
with Christian characters
facing the challenges
of life and love
in today's world.

**AVAILABLE IN REGULAR
AND LARGER-PRINT FORMATS.**

For exciting stories that reflect traditional values,
visit:
www.ReaderService.com

ReaderService.com

Manage your account online!

- Review your order history
- Manage your payments
- Update your address

*We've designed
the Harlequin® Reader Service
website just for you.*

Enjoy all the features!

- Reader excerpts from any series
- Respond to mailings and
  special monthly offers
- Discover new series available to you
- Browse the Bonus Bucks catalog
- Share your feedback

Visit us at:
ReaderService.com